Tam o' the Scoots by Edgar Wallace

Richard Horatio Edgar Wallace was born on the 1st April 1875 in Greenwich, London. Leaving school at 12 because of truancy, by the age of fifteen he had experience; selling newspapers, as a worker in a rubber factory, as a shoe shop assistant, as a milk delivery boy and as a ship's cook.

By 1894 he was engaged but broke it off to join the Infantry being posted to South Africa. He also changed his name to Edgar Wallace which he took from Lew Wallace, the author of *Ben-Hur*.

In Cape Town in 1898 he met Rudyard Kipling and was inspired to begin writing. His first collection of ballads, *The Mission that Failed!* was enough of a success that in 1899 he paid his way out of the armed forces in order to turn to writing full time.

By 1904 he had completed his first thriller, *The Four Just Men*. Since nobody would publish it he resorted to setting up his own publishing company which he called Tallis Press.

In 1911 his Congolese stories were published in a collection called *Sanders of the River*, which became a bestseller. He also started his own racing papers, *Bibury's* and *R. E. Walton's Weekly*, eventually buying his own racehorses and losing thousands gambling. A life of exceptionally high income was also mirrored with exceptionally large spending and debts.

Wallace now began to take his career as a fiction writer more seriously, signing with Hodder and Stoughton in 1921. He was marketed as the 'King of Thrillers' and they gave him the trademark image of a trilby, a cigarette holder and a yellow Rolls Royce. He was truly prolific, capable not only of producing a 70,000 word novel in three days but of doing three novels in a row in such a manner. It was estimated that by 1928 one in four books being read was written by Wallace, for alongside his famous thrillers he wrote variously in other genres, including science fiction, non-fiction accounts of WWI which amounted to ten volumes and screen plays. Eventually he would reach the remarkable total of 170 novels, 18 stage plays and 957 short stories.

Wallace became chairman of the Press Club which to this day holds an annual Edgar Wallace Award, rewarding 'excellence in writing'.

Diagnosed with diabetes his health deteriorated and he soon entered a coma and died of his condition and double pneumonia on the 7th of February 1932 in North Maple Drive, Beverly Hills. He was buried near his home in England at Chalklands, Bourne End, in Buckinghamshire.

Index of Contents

CHAPTER I

THE CASE OF LASKY

Lieutenant Bridgeman went out over the German line and "strafed" a depot. He stayed a while to locate a new gun position and was caught between three strong batteries of Archies.

"Reports?" said the wing commander. "Well, Bridgeman isn't back and Tam said he saw him nose-dive behind the German trenches."

So the report was made to Headquarters and Headquarters sent forward a long account of air flights for publication in the day's communiqué, adding, "One of our machines did not return."

"But, A' doot if he's killit," said Tam; "he flattened oot before he reached airth an' flew aroond a bit. Wi' ye no ask Mr. Lasky, sir-r, he's just in?"

Mr. Lasky was a bright-faced lad who, in ordinary circumstances, might have been looking forward to his leaving-book from Eton, but now had to his credit divers bombed dumps and three enemy airmen.

He met the brown-faced, red-haired, awkwardly built youth whom all the Flying Corps called "Tam."

"Ah, Tam," said Lasky reproachfully, "I was looking for you—I wanted you badly."

Tam chuckled.

"A' thocht so," he said, "but A' wis not so far frae the aerodrome when yon feller chased you—"

"I was chasing him!" said the indignant Lasky.

"Oh, ay?" replied the other skeptically. "An' was ye wantin' the Scoot to help ye chase ain puir wee Hoon? Sir-r, A' think shame on ye for misusin' the puir laddie."

"There were four," protested Lasky.

"And yeer gun jammed, A'm thinkin', so wi' rair presence o' mind, ye stood oop in the fuselage an' hit the nairest representative of the Imperial Gairman Air Sairvice a crack over the heid wi' a spanner."

A little group began to form at the door of the mess-room, for the news that Tam the Scoot was "up" was always sufficient to attract an audience. As for the victim of Tam's irony, his eyes were dancing with glee.

"Dismayed or frichtened by this apparition of the supermon i' the air-r," continued Tam in the monotonous tone he adopted when he was evolving one of his romances, "the enemy fled, emittin' spairks an' vapair to hide them from the veegilant ee o' young Mr. Lasky, the Boy Avenger, oor the Terror o' the Fairmament. They darted heether and theether wi' their remorseless pairsuer on their heels an' the seenister sound of his bullets whistlin' in their lugs. Ain by ain the enemy is defeated, fa'ing like Lucifer in a flamin' shrood. Soodenly Mr. Lasky turns verra pale. Heavens! A thocht has strook him. Where is Tam the Scoot? The horror o' the thocht leaves him braithless; an' back he tairns an' like a hawk deeps sweeftly but gracefully into the aerodrome— saved!"

"Bravo, Tam!" They gave him his due reward with great handclapping and Tam bowed left and right, his forage cap in his hand.

"Folks," he said, "ma next pairformance will be duly annoonced."

Tam came from the Clyde. He was not a ship-builder, but was the assistant of a man who ran a garage and did small repairs. Nor was he, in the accepted sense of the word, a patriot, because he did not enlist at the beginning of the war. His boss suggested he should, but Tam apparently held other views, went into a shipyard and was "badged and reserved."

They combed him out of that, and he went to another factory, making a false statement to secure the substitution of the badge he had lost. He was unmarried and had none dependent on him, and his landlord, who had two sons fighting, suggested to Tam that though he'd hate to lose a good lodger, he didn't think the country ought to lose a good soldier.

Tam changed his lodgings.

He moved to Glasgow and was insulted by a fellow workman with the name of coward. Tam hammered his fellow workman insensible and was fired forthwith from his job.

Every subterfuge, every trick, every evasion and excuse he could invent to avoid service in the army, he invented. He simply did not want to be a soldier. He believed most passionately that the war had been started with the sole object of affording his enemies opportunities for annoying him.

Then one day he was sent on a job to an aerodrome workshop. He was a clever mechanic and he had mastered the intricacies of the engine which he was to repair, in less than a day.

He went back to his work very thoughtfully, and the next Sunday he bicycled to the aerodrome in his best clothes and renewed his acquaintance with the mechanics.

Within a week, he was wearing the double-breasted tunic of the Higher Life. He was not a good or a tractable recruit. He hated discipline and regarded his superiors as less than equals—but he was an enthusiast.

When Pangate, which is in the south of England, sent for pilots and mechanics, he accompanied his officer and flew for the first time in his life.

In the old days he could not look out of a fourth-floor window without feeling giddy. Now he flew over England at a height of six thousand feet, and was sorry when the journey came to an end. In a few months he was a qualified pilot, and might have received a commission had he so desired.

"Thank ye, sir-r," he said to the commandant, "but ye ken weel A'm no gentry. M' fairther was no believer in education, an' whilst ither laddies were livin' on meal at the University A' was airning ma' salt at the Govan Iron Wairks. A'm no' a society mon ye ken—A'd be usin' the wrong knife to eat wi' an' that would bring the coorp into disrepute."

His education had, as a matter of fact, been a remarkable one. From the time he could read, he had absorbed every boy's book that he could buy or borrow. He told a friend of mine that when he enlisted he handed to the care of an acquaintance over six hundred paper-covered volumes which surveyed the world of adventure, from the Nevada of Deadwood Dick to the Australia of Jack Harkaway. He knew the stories by heart, their phraseology and their construction, and was wont at times, half in earnest, half in dour fun (at his own expense), to satirize every-day adventures in the romantic language of his favorite authors.

He was regarded as the safest, the most daring, the most venomous of the scouts—those swift-flying spitfires of the clouds—and enjoyed a fame among the German airmen which was at once flattering and ominous. Once they dropped a message into the aerodrome. It was short and humorous, but there was enough truth in the message to give it a bite:

Let us know when Tam is buried, we would a wreath subscribe.

Officers, German Imperial Air Service. Section—Nothing ever pleased Tam so much as this unsolicited testimonial to his prowess.

He purred for a week. Then he learned from a German prisoner that the author of the note was the flyer of a big Aviatic, and went and killed him in fair fight at a height of twelve thousand feet.

"It was an engrossin' an' thrillin' fight," explained Tam; "the bluid was coorsin' in ma veins, ma hairt was palpitatin' wi' suppressed emotion. Roond an' roond ain another the dauntless airmen caircled, the noo above, the noo below the ither. Wi' supairb resolution Tam o' the Scoots nose-dived for the wee feller's tail, loosin' a drum at the puir body as he endeavoured to escape the lichtenin' swoop o' the intrepid Scotsman. Wi' matchless skeel, Tam o' the Scoots banked over an' brocht the gallant miscreant to terra firma —puir laddie! If he'd kept ben the hoose he'd no' be lyin' deid the nicht. God rest him!"

You might see Tam in the early morning, when the world was dark and only the flashes of guns revealed the rival positions, poised in the early sun, fourteen thousand feet in the air, a tiny spangle of white, smaller in magnitude than the fading stars. He seems motionless, though you know that he is traveling in big circles at seventy miles an hour.

He is above the German lines and the fleecy bursts of shrapnel and the darker patches where high explosive shells are bursting beneath him, advertise alike his temerity and the indignation of the enemy.

What is Tam doing there so early?

There has been a big raid in the dark hours; a dozen bombing machines have gone buzzing eastward to a certain railway station where the German troops waited in readiness to reinforce either A or B fronts. If you look long, you see the machines returning, a group of black specks in the morning sky. The Boches' scouts are up to attack—the raiders go serenely onward, leaving the exciting business of duel à l'outrance to the nippy fighting machines which fly above each flank. One such fighter throws himself at three of the enemy, diving, banking, climbing, circling and all the time firing "ticka—ticka—ticka—ticka!" through his propellers.

The fight is going badly for the bold fighting machine, when suddenly like a hawk, Tam o' the Scoots sweeps upon his prey. One of the enemy side-slips, dives and streaks to the earth, leaving a cloud of smoke to mark his unsubstantial path. As for the others, they bank over and go home. One falls in spirals within the enemy's lines. Rescuer and rescued land together. The fighting-machine pilot is Lieutenant Burnley; the observer, shot through the hand, but cheerful, is Captain Forsyn.

"Did ye no' feel a sense o' gratitude to the Almighty when you kent it were Tam sittin' aloft like a wee angel?"

"I thought it was a bombing machine that had come back," said Burnley untruthfully.

"Did ye hear that, sir-rs?" asked Tam wrathfully. "For a grown officer an' gentleman haulding the certeeficate of the Royal Flying Coorp, to think ma machine were a bomber! Did ye no' look oop an' see me? Did ye no' look thankfully at yeer obsairvor, when, wi' a hooricane roar, the Terror of the Air-r hurtled across the sky—'Saved!' ye said to yersel'; 'saved — an' by Tam! What can I do to shaw ma appreciation of the hero's devotion? Why!' ye said to yersel', soodenly, 'Why! A'll gi' him a box o' seegairs sent to me by ma rich uncle fra' Glasgae—!'"

"You can have two cigars, Tam—I'll see you to the devil before I give you any more—I only had fifty in the first place."

"Two's no' many," said Tam calmly, "but A've na doot A'll enjoy them wi' ma educated palate better than you, sir-r—seegairs are for men an' no' for bairns, an' ye'd save yersel' an awfu' feelin' o' seekness if ye gave me a'."

Tam lived with the men—he had the rank of sergeant, but he was as much Tam to the private mechanic as he was to the officers. His pay was good and sufficient. He had shocked that section of the Corps Comforts Committee which devoted its energies to the collection and dispatch of literature, by requesting that a special effort be made to keep him supplied "wi' th' latest bluids." A member of the Committee with a sneaking regard for this type of literature took it upon himself to ransack London for penny dreadfuls, and Tam received a generous stock with regularity.

"A'm no' so fond o' th' new style," he said; "the detective stoory is verra guid in its way for hame consumption, but A' prefair the mair preemative discreeptions, of how that grand mon, Deadwood Dick, foiled the machinations of Black Peter, the Scoorge of Hell Cañon. A've no soort o' use for the new kind o' stoory—the love-stoories aboot mooney. Ye ken the soort: Harild is feelin' fine an' anxious aboot Lady Gwendoline's bairthmark: is she the rechtfu' heir? Oh, Heaven help me to solve the meestry! (To be continued in oor next.) A'm all for bluid an' fine laddies wi' a six-shooter in every hand an' a bowie-knife in their teeth—it's no' so intellectual, but, mon, it's mair human!"

Tam was out one fine spring afternoon in a one-seater Morane. He was on guard watching over the welfare of two "spotters" who were correcting the fire of a "grandmother" battery. There was a fair breeze blowing from the east, and it was bitterly cold, but Tam in his leather jacket, muffled to the eyes, and with his hands in fur-lined gloves and with the warmth from his engine, was comfortable without being cozy.

Far away on the eastern horizon he saw a great cloud. It was a detached and imperial cumulus, a great frothy pyramid that sailed in majestic splendor. Tam judged it to be a mile across at its base and calculated its height, from its broad base to its feathery spirelike apex, at another mile.

"There's an awfu' lot of room in ye," he thought.

It was moving slowly toward him and would pass him at such a level that did he explore it, he would enter half-way between its air foundation and its peak.

He signaled with his wireless, "Am going to explore cloud," and sent his Morane climbing.

He reached the misty outskirts of the mass and began its encirclement, drawing a little nearer to its center with every circuit. Now he was in a white fog which afforded him only an occasional glimpse of the earth. The fog grew thicker and darker and he returned again to the outer edge because there would be no danger in the center. Gently he declined his elevator and sank to a lower level. Then suddenly, beneath him, a short shape loomed through the mist and vanished in a flash. Tam had a tray of bombs under the fuselage— something in destructive quality between a Mills grenade and a three-inch shell.

He waited...

Presently—swish! They were circling in the opposite direction to Tam, which meant that the object passed him at the rate of one hundred and forty miles an hour. But he had seen the German coming... Something dropped from the fuselage, there was the rending crash of an explosion and Tam dropped a little, swerved to the left and was out in clear daylight in a second.

Back he streaked to the British lines, his wireless working frantically.

"Enemy raiding squadron in cloud—take the edge a quarter up."

He received the acknowledgment and brought his machine around to face the lordly bulk of the cumulus.

Then the British Archies began their good work.

Shrapnel and high explosives burst in a storm about the cloud. Looking down he saw fifty stabbing pencils of flame flickering from fifty A-A guns. Every available piece of anti-aircraft artillery was turned upon the fleecy mass.

As Tam circled he saw white specks rising swiftly from the direction of the aerodrome and knew that the fighting squadron, full of fury, was on its way up. It had come to be a tradition in the wing that Tam had the right of initiating all attack, and it was a right of which he was especially jealous. Now, with the great cloud disgorging its shadowy guests, he gave a glance at his Lewis gun and drove straight for his enemies. A bullet struck the fuselage and ricocheted past his ear; another ripped a hole in the canvas of his wing. He looked up. High above him, and evidently a fighting machine that had been hidden in the upper banks of the cloud, was a stiffly built Fokker.

"Noo, lassie!" said Tam and nose-dived.

Something flashed past his tail, and Tam's machine rocked like a ship at sea. He flattened out and climbed. The British Archies had ceased fire and the fight was between machine and machine, for the squadron was now in position. Tam saw Lasky die and glimpsed the flaming wreck of the boy's machine as it fell, then he found himself attacked on two sides. But he was the swifter climber—the faster mover. He shot impartially left and right and below —there was nothing above him after the first surprise. Then something went wrong with his engines—they missed, started, missed again, went on —then stopped.

He had turned his head for home and begun his glide to earth.

He landed near a road by the side of which a Highland battalion was resting and came to ground without mishap. He unstrapped himself and descended from the fuselage slowly, stripped off his gloves and walked to where the interested infantry were watching him.

"Where are ye gaun?" he asked, for Tam's besetting vice was an unquenchable curiosity.

"To the trenches afore Masille, sir-r," said the man he addressed.

"Ye'll no' be callin' me 'sir-r,'" reproved Tam. "A'm a s-arrgent. Hoo lang will ye stay in the trenches up yon?"

"Foor days, Sergeant," said the man.

"Foor days—guid Lord!" answered Tam. "A' wouldn't do that wairk for a thoosand poonds a week."

"It's no' so bad," said half-a-dozen voices.

"Ut's verra, verra dangerous," said Tam, shaking his head. "A'm thankitfu' A'm no' a soldier—they tried haird to make me ain, but A' said, 'Noo, laddie—gie me a job—'"

"Whoo!"

A roar like the rush of an express train through a junction, and Tam looked around in alarm. The enemy's heavy shell struck the ground midway between him and his machine and threw up a great column of mud.

"Mon!" said Tam in alarm. "A' thocht it were goin' straicht for ma wee machine."

"What happened to you, Tam?" asked the wing commander.

Tam cleared his throat.

"Patrollin' by order the morn," he said, "ma suspeecions were aroused by the erratic movements of a graund clood. To think, wi' Tam the Scoot, was to act. Wi'oot a thocht for his ain parrsonal safety, the gallant laddie brocht his machine to the clood i' question, caircling through its oombrageous depths. It was a fine gay sicht—aloon i' th' sky, he ventured into the air-r-lions' den. What did he see? The clood was a nest o' wee horrnets! Slippin' a bomb he dashed madly back to the ooter air-r sendin' his S. O. S. wi' baith hands—thanks to his—"

He stopped and bit his lip thoughtfully.

"Come, Tam!" smiled the officer, "that's a lame story for you."

"Oh, ay," said Tam. "A'm no' in the recht speerit—Hoo mony did we lose?"

"Mr. Lasky and Mr. Brand," said the wing commander quietly.

"Puir laddies," said Tam. He sniffed. "Mr. Lasky was a bonnie lad — A'll ask ye to excuse me, Captain Thompson, sir-r. A'm no feelin' verra weel the day—ye've no a seegair aboot ye that ye wilna be wantin'?"

CHAPTER II

PUPPIES OF THE PACK

Tam was not infallible, and the working out of his great "thochts" did not always justify the confidence which he reposed in them. His idea of an "invisible aeroplane," for example, which was to be one painted sky blue that would "hairmonise wi' the blaw skies," was not a success, nor was his scheme for the creation of artificial clouds attended by any encouraging results. But Tam's "Attack Formation for Bombing Enemy Depots" attained to the dignity of print, and was confidentially circulated in French, English, Russian, Italian, Serbian, Japanese and Rumanian.

The pity is that a Scottish edition was not prepared in Tam's own language; and Captain Blackie, who elaborated Tam's rough notes and condensed into a few lines Tam's most romantic descriptions, had suggested such an edition for very private circulation.

It would have begun somewhat like this:

"The Hoon or Gairman is a verra bonnie fichter, but he has nae ineetiative. He squints oop in the morn an' he speers a fine machine ower by his lines.

"'Hoot!' says he, 'yon wee feller is Scottish, A'm thinkin'—go you, Fritz an' Hans an' Carl an' Heinrich, an' strafe the puir body.'

"'Nay,' says his oonder lootenant. 'Nein,' he says, 'ye daunt knaw what ye're askin', Herr Lootenant.'

"'What's wrong wi' ye?' says the oberlootenant. 'Are ye Gairman heroes or just low-doon Austreens that ye fear ain wee bairdie?'

"'Lootenant,' say they, 'yon feller is Tam o' the Scoots, the Brigand o' the Stars!'

"'Ech!' he says. 'Gang oop, ain o' ye, an' ask the lad to coom doon an' tak' a soop wi' us—we maun keep on the recht side o' Tam!'"

All this and more would have gone to form the preliminary chapter of the true version of Tam's code of attack.

"He's a rum bird, is Tam," said Captain Blackie at breakfast; "he brought down von Zeidlitz yesterday."

"Is von Zeidlitz down?" demanded half a dozen voices, and Blackie nodded.

"He was a good, clean fighter," said young Carter regretfully. "When did you hear this, sir?"

"This morning, through H. Q. Intelligence."

"Tam will be awfully bucked," said somebody. "He was complaining yesterday that life was getting too monotonous. By the way, we ought to drop a wreath for poor old von Zeidlitz."

"Tam will do it with pleasure," said Blackie; "he always liked von Zeidlitz—he called him 'Fritz Fokker' ever since the day von Zeidlitz nearly got Tam's tail down."

An officer standing by the window with his hands thrust into his pockets called over his shoulder:

"Here comes Tam."

The thunder and splutter of the scout's engine came to them faintly as Tam's swift little machine came skimming across the broad ground of the aerodrome and in a few minutes Tam was walking slowly toward the office, stripping his gloves as he went.

Blackie went out to him.

"Hello, Tam—anything exciting?"

Tam waved his hand—he never saluted.

"Will ye gang an' tak' a look at me eenstruments?" he asked mysteriously.

"Why, Tam?"

"Will ye, sir-r?"

Captain Blackie walked over to the machine and climbed up into the fuselage. What he saw made him gasp, and he came back to where Tam was standing, smug and self-conscious.

"You've been up to twenty-eight thousand feet, Tam?" asked the astonished Blackie. "Why, that is nearly a record!"

"A' doot ma baromeeter," said Tam; "if A' were no' at fochty thousand, A'm a Boche."

Blackie laughed.

"You're not a Boche, Tam," he said, "and you haven't been to forty thousand feet—no human being can rise eight miles. To get up five and a half miles is a wonderful achievement. Why did you do it?"

Tam grinned and slapped his long gloves together.

"For peace an' quiet," he said. "A've been chased by thairty air Hoons that got 'twixt me an' ma breakfast, so A' went oop a bit an' a bit more an' two fellers came behint me. There's an ould joke that A've never understood before—'the higher the fewer'—it's no' deefficult to understand it noo."

"You got back all right, anyhow," said Blackie.

"Aloon i' the vast an' silent spaces of the vaulted heavens," said Tam in his sing-song tones which invariably accompanied his narratives, "the Young Avenger of the Cloods, Tam the Scoot, focht his ficht. Attacked by owerwhelmin' foorces, shot at afore an' behint, the noble laddie didna lose his nairve. Mutterin' a brief—a verra brief—prayer that the Hoons would be strafed, he climbt an' climbt till he could 'a' strook a match on the moon. After him wi' set lips an' flashin' een came the bluidy-minded ravagers of Belgium, Serbia an'—A'm afreed—Roomania. Theer bullets whistled aboot his lugs but,

"His eyes were bricht,
His hairt were licht,
For Tam the Scoot was fu' o' ficht—"

"That's a wee poem A' made oop oot o' ma ain heid, Captain, at a height of twenty-three thoosand feet. A'm thinkin' it's the highest poem in the wairld."

"And you're not far wrong—well, what happened?"

"A' got hame," said Tam grimly, "an' ain o' yon Hoons did no' get hame. Mon! It took him an awfu' long time to fa'!"

He went off to his breakfast and later, when Blackie came in search for him, he found him lying on his bed smoking a long black cigar, his eyes glued to the pages of "Texas Tom, or the Road Agent's Revenge."

"I forgot to tell you, Tam," said Captain Blackie, "that von Zeidlitz is down."

"Doon?" said Tam, "'Fritz Fokker' doon? Puir laddie! He were a gay fichter—who strafft him?"

"You did—he was the man you shot down yesterday."

Tam's eyes were bright with excitement.

"Ye're fulin' me noo?" he asked eagerly. "It wisna me that straffit him? Puir auld Freetz! It were a bonnie an' a carefu' shot that got him. He wis above me, d'ye ken? 'Ah naw!' says I. 'Ye'll no try that tailbitin' trick on Tam,' says I; 'naw, Freetz—!' An' I maneuvered to miss him. I put a drum into him at close range an' the puir feller side-slippit an' nose-dived. Noo was it Freetz, then? Weel, weel!"

"We want you to take a wreath over—he'll be buried at Ludezeel."

"With the verra greatest pleasure," said Tam heartily, "and if ye'll no mind, Captain, A'd like to compose a wee vairse to pit in the box."

For two hours Tam struggled heroically with his composition. At the end of that time he produced with awkward and unusual diffidence a poem written in his sprawling hand and addressed:

Dedication to Mr. von Sidlits By Tam of the Scoots

"I'll read you the poem, Captain Blackie, sir-r," said Tam nervously, and after much coughing he read:

"A graund an' nooble clood Was the flyin' hero's shrood Who dies at half- past seven And he verra well desairves The place that God resairves For the men who die in Heaven.

"A've signed it, 'Kind regards an' deepest sympathy wi' a' his loved ains,'" said Tam. "A' didna say A' killit him—it would no be delicate."

The wreath in a tin box, firmly corded and attached to a little parachute, was placed in the fuselage of a small Morane—his own machine being in the hands of the mechanics—and Tam climbed into the seat. In five minutes he was pushing up at the steep angle which represented the extreme angle at which a man can fly. Tam never employed a lesser one.

He had learnt just what an aeroplane could do, and it was exactly all that he called for. Soon he was above the lines and was heading for Ludezeel. Archies blazed and banged at him, leaving a trail of puff balls to mark his course; an enemy scout came out of the clouds to engage him and was avoided, for the corps made it a point of honor not to fight when engaged on such a mission as was Tam's.

Evidently the enemy scout realized the business of this lone British flyer and must have signaled his views to the earth, for the anti-aircraft batteries suddenly ceased fire, and when, approaching Ludezeel, Tam sighted an enemy squadron engaged in a practise flight, they opened out and made way for him, offering no molestation.

Tam began to plane down. He spotted the big white-speckled cemetery and saw a little procession making its way to the grounds. He came down to a thousand feet and dropped his parachute. He saw it open and sail earthward and then some one on the ground waved a white handkerchief.

"Guid," said Tam, and began to climb homeward.

The next day something put out of action the engine of that redoubtable fighter, Baron von Hansen-Bassermann, and he planed down to the British aerodrome with his machine flaming.

A dozen mechanics dashed into the blaze and hauled the German to safety, and, beyond a burnt hand and a singed mustache, he was unharmed.

Lieutenant Baron von Hansen-Bassermann was a good-looking youth. He was, moreover, an undergraduate of Oxford University and his English was perfect.

"Hard luck, sir," said Blackie, and the baron smiled.

"Fortunes of war. Where's Tam?" he asked.

"Tam's up-stairs somewhere," said Blackie. He looked up at the unflecked blue of the sky, shading his eyes. "He's been gone two hours."

The baron nodded and smiled again.

"Then it was Tam!" he said. "I thought I knew his touch—does he 'loop' to express his satisfaction?"

"That's Tam!" said a chorus of voices.

"He was sitting in a damp cloud waiting for me," said the baron ruefully. "But who was the Frenchman with him?"

Blackie looked puzzled.

"Frenchman? There isn't a French machine within fifty miles; did he attack you, too?"

"No—he just sat around watching and approving. I had the curious sense that I was being butchered to make a Frenchman's holiday. It is curious how one gets those quaint impressions in the air—it is a sort of ninth sense. I had a feeling that Tam was 'showing off'—in fact, I knew it was Tam, for that reason."

"Come and have some breakfast before you're herded into captivity with the brutal soldiery," said Blackie, and they all went into the mess-room together, and for an hour the room rang with laughter, for both the baron and Captain Blackie were excellent raconteurs.

Tam, when he returned, had little to say about his mysterious companion in the air. He thought it was a "French laddie." Nor had he any story to tell about the driving down of the baron's machine. He could only say that he "kent" the baron and had met his Albatross before. He called him the "Croon Prince" because the black crosses painted on his wings were of a more elaborate design than was usual.

"You might meet the baron, Tam," said the wing commander. "He's just off to the Cage, and he wants to say 'How-d'-ye-do.'"

Tam met the prisoner and shook hands with great solemnity.

"Hoo air ye, sir-r?" he asked with admirable sang-froid. "A' seem to remember yer face though A' hae no' met ye—only to shoot at, an' that spoils yeer chance o' gettin' acquainted wi' a body."

"I think we've met before," said the baron with a grim little smile. "Oh, before I forget, we very much appreciated your poem, Tam; there are lines in it which were quite beautiful."

Tam flushed crimson with pleasure.

"Thank ye, sir-r," he blurted. "Ye couldna' 'a' made me more pleased —even if A' killit ye."

The baron threw back his head and laughed.

"Good-by, Tam—take care of yourself. There's a new man come to us who will give you some trouble."

"It's no' Mister MacMuller?" asked Tam eagerly.

"Oh—you've heard of Captain Müller?" asked the prisoner interestedly.

"Haird?—good Lord, mon—sir-r, A' mean—look here!"

He put his hand in his pocket and produced a worn leather case. From this he extracted two or three newspaper cuttings and selected one, headed "German Official."

"'Captain Muller,'" read Tam, "'yesterday shot doon his twenty-sixth aeroplane.'"

"That's Müller," said the other carefully. "I can tell you no more —except look after yourself."

"Ha'e na doot aboot that, sir-r," said Tam with confidence.

He went up that afternoon in accordance with instructions received from headquarters to "search enemy territory west of a line from Montessier to St. Pierre le Petit."

He made his search, and sailed down with his report as the sun reached the horizon.

"A verra quiet joorney," he complained, "A' was hopin' for a squint at Mr. MacMuller, but he was sleeping like a doormoose—A' haird his snoor risin' to heaven an' ma hairt wis sick wi' disappointed longin'. 'Hoo long,' A' says, 'hoo long will ye avoid the doom Tam o' the Scoots has marked ye doon for?' There wis naw reply."

"I've discovered Tam's weird pal," said Blackie, coming into the mess before lunch the next day. "He is Claude Beaumont of the American Squadron —Lefèvre, the wing commander, was up to-day. Apparently Beaumont is an exceedingly rich young man who has equipped a wing with its own machines, hangars and repair-shop, and he flies where he likes. Look at 'em!"

They crowded out with whatever glasses they could lay their hands upon and watched the two tiny machines that circled and dipped, climbed and banked about one another.

First one would dart away with the other in pursuit, then the chaser, as though despairing of overtaking his quarry, would turn back. The "hare" would then turn and chase the other.

"Have you ever seen two puppies at play?" asked Blackie. "Look at Tam chasing his tail—and neither man knows the other or has ever looked upon his face! Isn't it weird? That's von Hansen-Bassermann's ninth sense. They can't speak—they can't even see one another properly and yet they're good pals— look at 'em. I've watched the puppies of the pack go on in exactly the same way."

"What is Tam supposed to be doing?"

"He's watching the spotters. Tam will be down presently and we'll ask David how he came to meet Jonathan—this business has been going on for weeks."

Tam had received the recall signal. Beneath him he saw the two "spotters" returning home, and he waved his hand to his sporting companion and came round in a little more than twice his own length. He saw his strange friend's hand raised in acknowledgment, and watched him turn for the south. Tam drove on for a mile, then something made him look back.

Above his friend was a glittering white dragon-fly, and as he looked the fly darted down at the American tail.

"Missed him!" said Tam, and swung round. He was racing with the wind at top speed and he must have been doing one hundred and twenty miles an hour, but for the fact that he was climbing at the extreme angle. He saw the dragon-fly loop and climb and the American swing about to attack.

But his machine was too slow—that Tam knew. Nothing short of a miracle could save the lower machine, for the enemy had again reached the higher position. So engrossed was he with his plan that he did not see Tam until the Scot was driving blindly to meet him—until the first shower from Tam's Lewis gun rained on wing and fuselage. The German swerved in his drive and missed his proper prey. Tam was behind him and above him, but in no position to attack. He could, and did fire a drum into the fleeing foeman, but none of the shots took effect.

"Tairn him, Archie!" groaned Tam, and as though the earth gunners had heard his plea, a screen of bursting shrapnel rose before the dragon-fly. He turned and nose-dived with Tam behind him, but now his nose was for home, and Tam, after a five-mile pursuit, came round and made for home also. Near his own lines he came up with the circling "Frenchman" and received his thanks — four fingers extended in the air—before the signaler, taking a route within the lines, streaked for home.

"Phew!" said Tam, shaking his head.

"Who were you chasing?" asked Blackie. "He can go!"

"Yon's MacMuller," said Tam, jerking his thumb at the eastern sky. "He's a verra likeable feller—but a wee bit too canny an' a big bit too fast. Captain Blackie, sir-r, can ye no get me a machine that can flee? Ma wee machine is no' unlike a hairse, but A'm wishfu' o' providin' the coorpse."

"You've got the fastest machine in France, Tam," said the captain.

Tam nodded.

"It's verra likely—she wis no' runnin' so sweet," he confessed. "But, mon! That Muller! He's a braw Hoon an' A'm encouraged by the fine things that the baron said aboot ma poetry. Ech! A've got a graund vairse in ma heid for Mr. Muller's buryin'! Hae ye a seegair aboot ye, Captain Blackie? A' gave ma case to the Duke of Argyle an' he has no' retairned it."

CHAPTER III

THE COMING OF MÜLLER

There arrived one day at the aerodrome a large packing-case addressed "Sergeant Tam." There was no surname, though there was no excuse for the timidity which stopped short at "Tam." The consignor might, at least, have ventured to add a tentative and inquiring "Mac?"

Tam took the case into his little "bunk" and opened it. The stripping of the rough outer packing revealed a suave, unpolished cedar cabinet with two doors and a key that dangled from one of the knobs. Tam opened the case after some consideration and disclosed shelf upon shelf tightly packed with bundles of rich, brown, fragrant cigars.

There was a card inscribed:

"Your friend in the Merman pusher."

"Who," demanded Tam, "is ma low acqueentance, who dispoorts himsel' in an oot-o'-date machine?"

Young Carter, who had come in to inspect the unpacking, offered a suggestion.

"Probably the French machine that is always coming over here to see you," he said, "Mr. Thiggamy-tight, the American."

"Ah, to be sure!" said Tam relieved. "A' thocht maybe the Kaiser had sent me droogged seegairs—A'm an awfu' thorn in the puir laddie's side. Ye may laugh, Mister Carter, but A' reca' a case wheer a bonnie detective wi' the same name as ye'sel', though A' doot if he wis related to ye, was foiled by the machinations o' Ferdie the Foorger at the moment o' his triumph by the lad gieing him a seegair soaked in laud'num an' chlorofor-rm!"

He took a bundle, slipped out two cigars, offered one to his officer, after a brief but baffling examination to discover which was the worse, and lit the other.

"They're no' so bad," he admitted, "but yeer ain seegairs never taste so bonnie as the seegairs yeer frien's loan ye."

"They came in time," said Carter; "we'd started a League for the Suppression of Cigar Cadging."

"Maybe ye thocht o' makin' me treesurer? Naw? Ah weel, a wee seegair is no muckle to gie a body wha's brocht fame an' honor to the Wing."

"I often wonder, Tam," said Carter, "how much you're joking and laughing at yourself when you're talking about 'Tam, the Terror of the Clouds,' and how much you're in earnest."

A fleeting smile flickered for a second about Tam's mouth and vanished.

"In all guid wairks of reference, fra' Auld Morre's Almanac to the Clyede River Time-Table," he said soberly, "it's written that a Scotsman canna joke. If A'd no talk about Tam—would ye talk aboot ye'sel's? Naw! Ye'd go oop an' doon, fichtin' an' deein' wi'oot a waird. If ye'll talk aboot ye'sel's A'll no talk aboot Tam. A' knaw ma duty, Mister Carter—A'm the offeecial boaster o' the wing an' the coor, an' whin they bring me doon wi' a bullet in ma heid, A' hope ye'll engage anither like me."

"There isn't another like you, Tam," laughed Carter.

"Ye dinna knaw Glasca,'" replied Tam darkly.

Lieutenant Carter went up on "a tour of duty" soon after and Tam was on the ground to watch his departure.

"Tam," he shouted, before the controls were in, "I liked that cigar —I'll take fifty from you to-night."

"Ower ma deid body," said Tam, puffing contentedly at the very last inch of his own; "the watch-wairds o' victory are 'threeft an' economy'!"

"I've warned you," roared Carter, for now the engine was going.

Tam nodded a smiling farewell as the machine skipped and ran over the ground before it swooped upward into space.

He went back to his room, but had hardly settled himself to the examination of a new batch of blood-curdling literature before Blackie strode in.

"Mr. Carter's down, Tam," he said.

"Doon!"

Tam jumped up, a frown on his face.

"Shot dead and fell inside our lines—go up and see if you can find Müller."

Tam dressed slowly. Behind the mask of his face, God knows what sorrow lay, for he was fond of the boy, as he had been fond of so many boys who had gone up in the joy and pride of their youth, and had earned by the supreme sacrifice that sinister line in the communiques: "One of our machines did not return."

He ranged the heavens that day seeking his man. He waited temptingly in reachable places and even lured one of his enemies to attack him.

"There's something down," said Blackie, as a flaming German aeroplane shot downward from the clouds. "But I'm afraid it's not Müller this time."

It was not. Tam returned morose and uncommunicative. His anger was increased when the intercepted wireless came to hand in the evening:

"Captain Müller shot down his twenty-seventh aeroplane."

That night, when the mess was sitting around after dinner, Tam appeared with a big armful of cigars.

"What's the matter with 'em?" asked Blackie in mock alarm.

"They're a' that Mister Carter bocht," said Tam untruthfully, "an' A' thocht ye'd wish to ha'e a few o' the laddie's seegairs."

Nobody was deceived. They pooled the cigars for the mess and Tam went back to his quarters lighter of heart. He slept soundly and was wakened an hour before dawn by his batman.

"'The weary roond, the deely task,'" quoted Tam, taking the steaming mug of tea from his servant's hands. "What likes the mornin', Horace?"

"Fine, Sergeant—clear sky an' all the stars are out."

"Fine for them," said Tam sarcastically, "they've nawthin' to do but be oot or in—A've no patience wi' the stars—puir silly bodies winkin' an' blinkin' an' doin' nae guid to mon or beastie—chuck me ma breeches an' let the warm watter rin in the bath."

In the gray light of dawn the reliefs stood on the ground, waiting for the word "go."

"A' wonder what ma frien' MacMuller is thinkin' the morn?" asked Tam; "wi' a wan face an' a haggaird een, he'll be takin' a moornfu' farewell o' the Croon Prince Ruppect.

"'Ye're a brave lad,' says the Croon Prince, 'but maybe Tam's awa'.'

"'Naw,' says MacMuller, shakin' his heid, 'A've a presentiment that Tam's no' awa'. He'll be oop-stairs waitin' to deal his feelon's-blow. Ech!' says Mister MacMuller, 'for why did I leave ma fine job at the gas-wairks to encoonter the perils an' advairsities of aerial reconnaissance?' he says. 'Well, I'll be gettin' alang, yeer Majesty or Highness—dawn't expect ma till ye see ma.'

"He moonts his graind machine an' soon the intrepid baird-man is soorin' to the skies. He looks oop—what is that seenister for-rm lairking in the cloods? It is Tam the Comet!"

"Up, you talkative devil," said Blackie pleasantly.

Tam rode upward at an angle which sent so great a pressure of air against him that he ached in back and arm and legs to keep his balance. It was as though he were leaning back without support, with great weights piled on his chest. He saw nothing but the pale blue skies and the fleecy trail of high clouds, heard nothing but the numbing, maddening roar of his engines.

He sang a little song to himself, for despite his discomfort he was happy enough. His eyes were for the engine, his ears for possible eccentricities of running. He was pushing a straight course and knew exactly where he was by a glance at his barometer. At six thousand feet he was behind the British lines at the Bois de Colbert, at seven thousand feet he should be over Nivelle- Ancre and should turn so that he reached his proper altitude at a point one mile behind the fire trenches and somewhere in the region of the Bois de Colbert again.

The aeronometer marked twelve thousand feet when he leveled the machine and began to take an interest in military affairs. The sky was clear of machines, with the exception of honest British spotters lumbering along like farm laborers to their monotonous toil. A gentlemanly fighting machine was doing "stunts" over by Serray and there was no sign of an enemy. Tam looked down. He saw a world of tiny squares intersected by thin white lines. These were main roads. He saw little dewdrops of water occurring at irregular intervals. They were really respectable-sized lakes.

Beneath him were two irregular scratches against the dull green-brown of earth that stretched interminably north and south. They ran parallel at irregular distances apart. Sometimes they approached so that it seemed that they touched. In other places they drew apart from one another for no apparent reason and there was quite a respectable distance of ground between them. These were the trench lines, and every now and again on one side or the other a puff of dirty brown smoke would appear and hang like a pall before the breeze sent it streaming slowly backward.

Sometimes the clouds of smoke would be almost continuous, but these shell- bursts were not confined to the front lines. From where Tam hung he could see billowing smoke clouds appear in every direction. Far behind the enemy's lines at the great road junctions, in the low-roofed billeting villages, on the single-track railways, they came and went.

The thunder of his engines drowned all sound so he could not hear the never-ceasing booming of the guns, the never-ending crash of exploding shell. Once he saw a heavy German shell in the air—he glimpsed it at that culminating point of its trajectory where the shell begins to lose its initial velocity and turns earthward again. It was a curious experience, which many airmen have had, and quite understandable, since the howitzer shell rises to a tremendous height before it follows the descending curve of its flight.

He paid a visit to the only cloud that had any pretensions to being a cloud, and found nothing. So he went over the German lines. He passed far behind the fighting front and presently came above a certain confusion of ground which marked an advance depot. He pressed his foot twice on a lever and circled. Looking down he saw two red bursts of flame and a mass of smoke. He did not hear the explosions of the bombs he had loosed, because it was impossible to hear anything but the angry "Whar-r-r—!" of his engines.

A belligerent is very sensitive over the matter of bombed depots, and Tam, turning homeward, looked for the machines which would assuredly rise to intercept him. Already the Archies were banging away at him, and a fragment of shell had actually struck his fuselage. But he was not bothering about Archies. He did swerve toward a battery skilfully hidden behind a hayrick and drop two hopeful bombs, but he scarcely troubled to make an inspection of the result.

Then before him appeared his enemy. Tam had the sun at his back and secured a good view of the Müller machine. It was the great white dragon-fly he had seen two days before. Apparently Müller had other business on hand. He was passing across Tam's course diagonally—and he was climbing.

Tam grinned. He was also pushing upward, for he knew that his enemy, seemingly oblivious to his presence, had sighted him and was getting into position to attack. Tam's engine was running beautifully, he could feel a subtle resolution in the "pull" of it; it almost seemed that this thing of steel was possessed of a soul all its own. He was keeping level with the enemy, on a parallel course which enabled him to keep his eye upon the redoubtable fighter.

Then, without warning, the German banked over and headed straight for Tam, his machine-gun stuttering. Tam turned to meet him. They were less than half a mile from each other and were drawing together at the rate of two hundred miles an hour. There were, therefore, just ten seconds separating them. What maneuver Müller intended is not clear. He knew—and then he realized in a flash what Tam was after.

Round he went, rocking like a ship at sea. A bullet struck his wheel and sent the smashed wood flying. He nose-dived for his own lines and Tam glared down after him.

Müller reached his aerodrome and was laughing quietly when he descended.

"I met Tam," he said to his chief; "he tried to ram me at sixteen thousand feet—Oh, yes. I came down, but—ich habe das nicht gewollt!—I did not will it!"

Tam returned to his headquarters full of schemes and bright "thochts."

"You drove him down?" said the delighted Blackie. "Why, Tam, it's fine! Müller never goes down—you've broken one of his traditions."

"A' wisht it was ain of his heids," said Tam. "A' thocht for aboot three seconds he was acceptin' the challenge o' the Glasca' Ganymede— A'm no' so sure o' Ganymede; A' got him oot of the sairculatin' library an' he was verra dull except the bit wheer he went oop in the air on the back of an eagle an' dropped his whustle. But MacMuller wasn't so full o' ficht as a' that."

He walked away, but stopped and came back.

"A'm a Wee Kirker," he said. "A' remembered it when A' met MacMuller. Though A'm no particular hoo A'm buried, A'm entitled to a Wee Kirk meenister. Mony's the time A've put a penny i' the collection. It sair grievit me to waste guid money, but me auld mither watchit me like a cat, an' 'twere as much as ma life was worth to pit it in ma breeches pocket."

Tam spent the flying hours of the next day looking for his enemy, but without result. The next day he again drew blank, and on the third day took part in an organized raid upon enemy communications, fighting his way back from the interior of Belgium single-handed, for he had allowed himself to be "rounded out" and had to dispose of two enemy machines before he could go in pursuit of the bombing squadrons. In consequence, he had to meet and reject the attentions of every ruffled enemy that the bombers and their bullies had fought in passing.

At five o'clock in the evening he dropped from the heavens in one straight plummet dive which brought him three miles in a little under one minute.

"Did you meet Müller?" asked Captain Blackie; "he's about —he shot down Mr. Grey this morning whilst you were away."

"Mr. Gree? Weel, weel!" said Tam, shaking, "puir soul—he wis a verra guid gentleman—wit' a gay young hairt."

"I hope Tam will pronounce my epitaph," said Blackie to Bolt, the observer; "he doesn't know how to think unkindly of his pals."

"Tam will get Müller," said Bolt. "I saw the scrap the other day —Tam was prepared to kill himself if he could bring him down. He was out for a collision, I'll swear, and Müller knew it and lost his nerve for the fight. That means that Müller is hating himself and will go running for Tam at the first opportunity."

"Tam shall have his chance. The new B. I. 6 is ready and Tam shall have it."

Now every airman knows the character of the old B. I. 5. She was a fast machine, could rise quicker than any other aeroplane in the world. She could do things which no other machine could do, and could also behave as no self- respecting aeroplane would wish to behave. For example, she was an involuntary "looper." For no apparent reason at all she would suddenly buck like a lunatic mustang. In these frenzies she would answer no appliance and obey no other mechanical law than the law of gravitation.

Tam had tried B. I. 5, and had lived to tell the story. There is a legend that he reached earth flying backward and upside down, but that is probably without foundation. Then an ingenious American had taken B. I. 5 in hand and had done certain things to her wings, her tail, her fuselage and her engine and from the chaos of her remains was born B. I. 6, not unlike her erratic mother in appearance, but viceless.

Tam learned of his opportunity without any display of enthusiasm.

"A' doot she's na guid," he said. "Captain Blackie, sir-r, A've got ma ain idea what B. I. stands for. It's no complimentary to the inventor. If sax is better, than A'm goin' to believe in an auld sayin'."

"What is that, Tam?"

"'Theer's safety in numbers,'" said Tam, "an' the while A'm on the subject of leeterature A'd like yeer opinion on a vairse A' made aboot Mr. MacMuller."

He produced a folded sheet of paper, opened it, and read,

"Amidst the seelance of the stars
He fell, yon dooty mon o' Mars.
The angels laffit
To see this gaillant baird-man die.
'At lairst! At lairst!' the angels cry,
'We've ain who'll teach us hoo to fly—
Thanks be, he's strafit!'"

"Fine," said Blackie with a smile, "but suppose you're 'strafit' instead?"

"Pit the wee pome on ma ain wreath," said Tam simply; "'t 'ill be true."

CHAPTER IV

THE STRAFING OF MÜLLER

On the earth, rain was falling from gray and gloomy clouds. Above those clouds the sun shone down from a blue sky upon a billowing mass that bore a resemblance to the uneven surface of a limitless plain of lather. High, but not too high above cloud-level, a big white Albatross circled serenely, its long, untidy wireless aerial dangling.

The man in the machine with receivers to his ears listened intently for the faint "H D" which was his official number. Messages he caught— mostly in English, for he was above the British lines.

"Nine—Four... Nine—four ... nine—four," called somebody insistently. That was a "spotter" signaling a correction of range, then... "Stop where you are ... KLBQ... Bad light... Signal to XO 73 last shot... Repeat your signal ... No... Bad light... Sorry—bad light... Stay where you are..."

He guessed some, could not follow others. The letter-groups were, of course, code messages indicating the distance shells were bursting from their targets. The apologies were easily explained, for the light was very bad indeed.

"Tam... Müller... Above... el."

The man in the machine tried the lock of his gun and began to get interested.

Now his eyes were fixed upon the rolling, iridescent cloud-mass below. From what point would the fighting machine emerge?

He climbed up a little higher to be on the safe side. Then, from a valley of mist half a mile away, a tiny machine shot up, shining like burnished silver in the rays of the afternoon sun, for Tam had driven up in a drizzle of rain, and wings and fuselage were soaking wet.

The watcher above rushed to the attack. He was perhaps a thousand yards above his enemy and had certain advantages—a fact which Tam realized. He ceased to climb, flattened and went skimming along the top of the cloud, darting here and there with seeming aimlessness. His pursuer rapidly reviewed the situation.

To dive down upon his prey would mean that in the event of missing his erratic moving foe, the attacker would plunge into the cloud fog and be at a disadvantage. At the same time, he would risk it. Suddenly up went his tail. But Tam had vanished in the mist, for as he saw the tail go up, he had followed suit, and nothing in the world dives like a B. I. 6.

No sooner was he out of sight of his attacker than he brought the nose of the machine up again and began a lightning climb to sunshine. He was the first to reach "open country" and he looked round for Müller.

That redoubtable fighter reappeared in front and below him and Tam dived for him. Müller's nose went down and back to his hiding-place he dived. Tam corrected his level and swooped upward again. There was no sign of Captain Müller. Tam cruised up and down, searching the cloud for his enemy.

He was doing three things at once: He was looking, he was fitting another drum to his gun, and he was controlling the flight of his machine, when "chk- chk-chk" said the wireless, and Tam listened, screwing his face into a grimace signifying at once the difficulty of hearing, and his apprehension that he might lose a word of what was to follow.

"L Q—L Q," said the receiver.

"Noo," said Tam in perplexity, "is 'L Q' meanin' that A' ocht to rin for ma life or is it 'continue the guid wairk'?"

Arguing that his work was invisible from the earth and that a more urgent interpretation was to be put upon the message, he turned westward and dived; not, however, before he had seen over his shoulder a dozen enemy machines come flashing up from the clouds.

"Haird cheese!" said Tam; "a' the auld cats aboot an' the wee moosie's awa'!"

He had intended going home, but a new and bright thought struck him. He turned his machine and pushed straight through the cloud the way he had come. He knew they had seen him disappearing and, airman like, they would remain awhile to bask in the sunlight and "dry off."

As a general rule Tam hated clouds. You could not tell whether you were flying right side up or upside down, and he had always a curious sense of nervousness that he would collide with something. Yet, for once, he drove through the swirling "smoke" with a sense of joyous anticipation, and presently began to rise gently, keeping his eyes aloft to detect the first thinning of the fog. Presently he saw the sunlight reflected on the upper stratas and began to climb steeply. His machine ripped out into the sun, a fierce, roaring little fury.

Not a hundred yards away was a fighting machine.

"Ticka—ticka—ticka—ticka—tick!" said Tam's machine-gun.

Tam's staring blue eyes were on the sights—he could not miss. The pilot went limp in his seat, the observer took his hand from his gun to grip the controls. Too late; the wide-winged fighter skidded like a motorbus on a greasy road and fell into the clouds sideways.

But now the enemy was coming at him from all points of the compass.

"Dinna let oor pairtin' grieve ye!" sang Tam and dropped straight through the clouds into the rain and a dim view of a bedraggled earth.

"There's Burley," said Blackie, clad in a long oilskin and a sou'wester as he checked off the home-coming adventurers. "Do you ever notice how his machine always looks lop-sided? There's Galbraith and Mosen—who's that fellow on the Morane? Oh, yes, that's Parker-Smith. H'm!"

"What's wrong?"

"Where's Tam—I hope those beggars didn't catch him— There he is, the devil!"

Tam was doing stunts. He was side-slipping, nose-diving and looping —he was, in fine, setting up all those stresses which a machine under extraordinary circumstances might have to endure.

"He always does that with a new machine, sir," said Captain Blackie's companion. "I've never understood why, because if he found a weak place, he'd be too dead for the information to be of any service to him."

Later, when Tam condescended to bring himself to earth, Blackie asked him.

"Why do you do fool stunts, Tam? The place to test the machine is on the ground?"

"Ye're wrong, sir-r," said Tam quietly; "the groond's a fine place to test a wee perambulator or a motor-car or a pair of buits—but it's no' the place to test an aeroplane. The aeroplane an' the submarine maun be tried oot in their native eelements."

"But suppose you did succeed in breaking something— and you went to glory?"

"Aye," said Tam quietly, "an' suppose A'm goin' oop wi' matchless coorage to save ma frien's frae the ravishin' Hoon an' ma machine plays hookey? Would it no' be worse for a' concairned, than if A' smash oop by mesel'?"

"Did you see Müller?"

"In the clouds. A' left him hauldin' a committee-meetin', Captain MacMuller in the cheer.

"'Resolvit,' says the cheerman, 'that this meetin', duly an' truly assembled, passes a hairty vote o' thanks to Tam o' the Scoots, the Mageecian o' the Air-r, for the grand fight he made against a superior enemy— Carried.

"'Resolvit,' says the cheerman, 'that we'll no' ta' onny more risk, but confine oor attentions to strafin' spotters—'

"Carried wi' acclamation. The meetin' then adjoorned to enquire after machine noomber sax, eight, sax, two, strafed in the execution of ma duty."

It seemed almost as though Tam's words were prophetic, for the next day Smyth and Curzon were attacked whilst "spotting" for the "heavies" and fell in flames in No-Man's Land. They got Smyth in during the night and rushed him back to a base hospital; but Curzon was dead before the machine reached the ground.

The same morning Tam read in the German "Official":

"In the course of the day Captain Müller shot down his thirtieth enemy aeroplane, which fell before the English lines."

"It were no' the English lines, but the Argyll an' Sootherland Hielanders' lines," complained Tam. "Thairty machines yon Muller ha' strafit. Weel, weel!"

He went to his room very thoughtful, and the day following, being an "off" day, he spent between the machine-shop and the hangar where the B. I. 6 reposed. It must never be forgotten that Tam was a born mechanician. To him the machine had a body, a soul, a voice, and a temperament. Noises which engines made had a peculiar significance to Tam. He not only could tell you how they were behaving, but how they would be likely to behave after two hours' running. He knew all the symptoms of their mysterious diseases and he was versed in their dietary. He "fed" his own engines, explored his own tanks, greased and cleaned with his own hands every delicate part of the frail machinery.

There was neither strut nor stay, bolt nor screw, that he did not know or had not studied, tested or replaced. He cleaned his own gun and examined, leather duster in hand, every round of ammunition he took up. He left little to chance and never went out to attack but with a "plan, an altairnitive plan an' — an open mind."

And now since Müller must be settled with, Tam was more than careful.

The difficulty about aeroplanes is that they look very much like one another. Tam fought indecisively three big white Albatross machines before a Fokker hawk darted down from the shelter of a cloud-wraith and revealed itself as the temporary preoccupation of Captain Müller.

The encounter may be told in Tam's own words.

"I' the ruthless pairsuit of his duty, Tam was patrollin' at a height o' twelve thoosand feet, his mind filled wi' beautifu' thochts aboot pay-day, when a cauld shiver passes doon the dauntless spine o' the wee hero. 'Tis a preemonition or warnin' o' peeril. He speers oop an' doon absint-mindedly fingerin' the mechanism of his seelver-plated Lewis gun. There was nawthing in sicht, nawthing to mar the glories of the morn. 'Can A' be mistaken?' asks Tam. 'Noo! A thoosand times noo!' an' wi' these fatefu' wairds, he began his peerilous climb. Maircifu' Heavens! What's yon? 'Tis the mad Muller! Sweeft as the eagle fa'ing upon his prey, fa's MacMuller, a licht o' joy in his een, his bullets twangin' like hairp-strings. But Tam the Tempest is no' bothered. Cal-lm an' a'most majeestic in his sang-frow—a French expression — he leps gaily to the fray—an' here A' am!"

"But, Tam," protested Galbraith, "that's a rotten story. What happened after the lep—did you get up to him?"

"A' didna lep oop," said Tam gravely; "A' lep doon—it wis no' the time to ficht—it wis the time to flee—an' A'm a fleein' mon."

That he would deliberately shrink an issue with his enemy was unthinkable. And yet he rather avoided than sought Müller after this encounter.

One afternoon he came to Galbraith's quarters. Galbraith was rich and young and a great sportsman.

"Can A' ha'e a waird wi' ye?" asked Tam mysteriously.

"Surely," said the boy. "Come in—you want a cigar, Tam!" he accused.

"Get awa' ahint me, Satan," said Tam piously. "A've gi'en oop cadgin' seegairs an' A' beg ye no' tae tempit a puir weak body. Just puit the box doon whair A' can reach it an' mebbe A'll help mesel' absintminded. A' came — mon, this is a bonnie smawk! Ye maun pay an awfu' lot for these. Twa sheelin's each! Ech! It's sinfu' wi' so many puir souls in need—A'll tak' a few wi' me when A' go, to distreebute to the sufferin' mechanics. Naw, it is na for seegairs A'm beggin', na this time—but ha'e ye an auld suit o' claes ye'll no be wantin'?"

"A suit? Good Lord, yes, Tam," said Galbraith, jumping down from the table on which he was seated. "Do you want it for yourself?"

"Well," replied Tam cautiously, "A' do an' A' doon't—it's for ma frien', Fitzroy McGinty, the celebrated MacMuller mairderer."

Galbraith looked at him with laughter in his eyes.

"Fitzroy McGinty? And who the devil is Fitzroy McGinty?"

Tam cleared his throat

"Ma frien' Fitzroy McGinty is, like Tam, an oornament o' the Royal Fleein' Coor. Oor hero was borr-rn in affluent saircumstances his faither bein' the laird o' Maclacity, his mither a Fitzroy o' Soosex. Fitz McGinty lived i' a ground castle wi' thoosands o' sairvants to wait on him, an' he ate his parritch wi' a deemond spune. A' seemed rawsy for the wee boy, but yin day, accused o' the mairder o' the butler an' the bairglary of his brithers' troosers, he rin frae hame, crossin' to Ameriky, wheer he foon' employment wi' a rancher as coo-boy. Whilst there, his naturally adventurous speerit brocht him into contact wi' Alkali Pete the Road-Agent—ye ken the feller that haulds oop the Deadville stage?"

"Oh, I ken him all right," said the patient Galbraith; "but, honestly, Tam—who is your friend?"

"Ma frien', Angus McCarthy?"

"You said Fitzroy McGinty just now."

"Oh, aye," said Tam hastily, "'twas ain of his assoomed names."

"You're a humbug—but here's the kit. Is that of use?"

"Aye."

Tam gathered the garments under his arm and took a solemn farewell.

"Ye'll be meetin' Rabbie again—A' means Angus, Mr. Galbraith —but A'd be glad if ye'd no mention to him that he's weerin' yeer claes."

He went to a distant store and for the rest of the day, with the assistance of a mechanic, he was busy creating the newest recruit to the Royal Flying Corps. Tam was thorough and inventive. He must not only stuff the old suit with wood shavings and straw, but he must unstuff it again, so that he might thread a coil of pliable wire to give the figure the necessary stiffness.

"Ye maun hae a backbone if ye're to be an obsairver, ma mannie," said Tam, "an' noo for yeer bonnie face—Horace, will ye pass me the plaister o' Paris an' A'll gi' ye an eemitation o' Michael Angy-low, the celebrated face- maker."

His work was interluded with comments on men and affairs—the very nature of his task brought into play that sense of humor and that stimulation of fancy to which he responded with such readiness.

"A' doot whither A'll gi'e ye a moostache," said Tam, surveying his handiwork, "it's no necessairy to a fleein'-mon, but it's awfu' temptin' to an airtist."

He scratched his head thoughtfully.

"Ye should be more tanned, Angus," he said and took up the varnish brush.

At last the great work was finished. The dummy was lifelike even outside of the setting which Tam had planned. From the cap (fastened to the plaster head by tacks) to the gloved hands, the figure was all that an officer of the R.F.C. might be, supposing he were pigeon-toed and limp of leg.

The next morning Tam called on Blackie in his office and asked to be allowed to take certain liberties with his machine, a permission which, when it was explained, was readily granted. He went up in the afternoon and headed straight for the enemy's lines. He was flying at a considerable height, and Captain Müller, who had been on a joy ride to another sector of the line and had descended to his aerodrome, was informed that a very high-flying spotter was treating Archie fire with contempt and had, moreover, dropped random bombs which, by the greatest luck in the world, had blown up a munition reserve.

"I'll go up and scare him off," said Captain Müller. He focussed a telescope upon the tiny spotter.

"It looks more like a fast scout than a spotter," he said, "yet there are obviously two men in her."

He went up in a steep climb, his powerful engines roaring savagely. It took him longer to reach his altitude than he had anticipated. He was still below the alleged spotter with its straw-stuffed observer when Tam dived for him.

All that the nursing of a highly trained mechanic could give to an engine, all of precision that a cold blue eye and a steady hand could lend to a machine-gun, all that an unfearing heart could throw into that one wild, superlative fling, Tam gave. The engine pulled to its last ounce, the wings and stays held to the ultimate stress.

"Tam!" said Müller to himself and smiled, for he knew that death had come.

He fired upward and banked over—then he waved his hand in blind salute, though he had a bullet in his heart and was one with the nothingness about him.

Tam swung round and stared fiercely as Müller's machine fell. He saw it strike the earth, crumple and smoke.

"Almichty God," said the lips of Tam, "look after that yin! He wis a bonnie fichter an' had a gay hairt, an' he knaws richt weel A' had no malice agin him—Amen!"

CHAPTER V

ANNIE—THE GUN

"A've noticed," said Tam, "a deesposition in writin' classes to omit the necessary bits of scenery that throw up the odious villainy of the factor, or the lonely vairtue of the Mill Girl. A forest maiden wi'oot the forest or a hard-workin' factory lass wi'oot a chimney-stalk, is no more convincin' than a seegair band wi'oot the seegair, or an empty pay envelope."

"Why this disquisition on the arts, Tam?" asked Captain Blackie testily.

Three o'clock in the morning, and freezing at that, a dark aerodrome and the ceaseless drum of guns— neither the time, the place nor the ideal accompaniment to philosophy, you might think. Blackie was as nervous as a squadron commander may well be who has sent a party on a midnight stunt, and finds three o'clock marked on the phosphorescent dial of his watch and not so much as a single machine in sight.

"Literature," said Tam easily, "is a science or a disease very much like airmanship. 'Tis all notes of excl'mation an' question mairks, with one full stop an' several semi-comatose crashes—!"

"Oh, for Heaven's sake, shut up, Tam!" said Blackie savagely. "Haven't you a cigar to fill that gap in your face?"

"Aye," said Tam calmly, "did ye no' smell it? It's one o' young Master Taunton's Lubricatos an' A'm smokin' it for an endurance test— they're no' so bad, remembering the inexperience an' youth o' ma wee frien'—"

Blackie turned.

"Tam," he said shortly, "I'm just worried sick about those fellows and I wish—"

"Oh, them," said Tam in an extravagant tone of surprise, "they're comin' back, Captain Blackie, sir-r—a' five, one with an engine that's runnin' no' so sweet—that'll be Mister Gordon's, A'm thinkin'."

Captain Blackie turned to the other incredulously.

"You can hear them?" he asked. "I hear nothing."

"It's the smell of Master Taunton's seegair in your ears," said Tam. "For the past five minutes A've been listenin' to the gay music of their tractors, bummin' like the mill hooter on a foggy morn—there they are!"

High in the dark heavens a tiny speck of red light glowed, lingered a moment and vanished. Then another, then a green that faded to white.

"Thank the Lord!" breathed Blackie. "Light up!"

"There's time," said Tam, "yon 'buses are fifteen thoosand up."

They came roaring and stuttering to earth, five monstrous shapes, and passed to the hands of their mechanics.

"Tam heard you," said Blackie to the young leader, stripping his gloves thoughtfully by the side of his machine. "Who had the engine trouble?"

"Gordon," chuckled the youth. "That 'bus is a—"

"Hec, sir!" said Tam and put his hands to his ears.

They had walked across to the commander's office.

"Well—what luck had you?" asked Blackie.

Lieutenant Taunton made a very wry face.

"I rather fancy we got the aerodrome—we saw something burning beautifully as we turned for home, but Fritz has a new searchlight installation and something fierce in the way of Archies. There's a new battery and unless I'm mistaken a new kind of gun—that's why we climbed. They angled the lights and got our range in two calendar seconds and they never left us alone. There was one gun in particular that was almost undodgable. I stalled and side-slipped, climbed and nose-dived, but the devil was always on the spot."

"Hum," said Blackie thoughtfully, "did you mark the new battery?"

"X B 84 as far as I could judge," said the other and indicated a tiny square on the big map which covered the side of the office; "it wasn't worth while locating, for I fancy that my particular friend was mobile— Tam, look out for the Demon Gunner of Bocheville."

"It is computed by state—by state—by fellers that coont," said Tam, "that it takes seven thoosand shells to hit a flyin'-man —by my own elaborate system of calculation, A' reckon that A've five thoosand shells to see before A' get the one that's marked wi' ma name an' address."

And he summarily dismissed the matter from his mind for the night. Forty- eight hours later he found the question of A-A gunnery a problem which was not susceptible to such cavalier treatment.

He came back to the aerodrome this afternoon, shooting down from a great height in one steep run, and found the whole of the squadron waiting for him. Tam descended from the fuselage very solemnly, affecting not to notice the waiting audience, and with a little salute, which was half a friendly nod, he would have made his way to squadron headquarters had not Blackie hailed him.

"Come on, Tam," he smiled. "Why this modesty?"

"Sir-r?" said Tam with well-simulated surprise.

"Let us hear about the gun."

"Ah, the gun," said Tam as though it were some small matter which he had overlooked in the greater business of the day. "Well, now, sir-r, that is some gun, and after A've had a sup o' tea A'll tell you the story of ma reckless exploits."

He walked slowly over to his mess, followed by the badinage of his superiors.

"You saw it, Austin, didn't you?" Blackie turned to the young airman.

"Oh, yes, sir. I was spotting for a howitzer battery and they were firing like a gas-pipe, by the way, right outside the clock—I can't make up my mind what is the matter with that battery."

"Never mind about the battery," interrupted Blackie; "tell us about Tam."

"I didn't see it all," said Austin, "and I didn't know it was Tam until later. The first thing I saw was one of our fellows 'zooming' up at a rare bat all on his lonely. I didn't take much notice of that. I thought it was one of our fellows on a stunt. But presently I could see Archie getting in his grand work. It was a battery somewhere on the Lille road, and it was a scorcher, for it got his level first pop. Instead of going on, the 'bus started circling as though he was enjoying the 'shrap' bath. As far as I could see there were four guns on him, but three of them were wild and late. You could see their bursts over him and under him, but the fourth was a terror. It just potted away, always at his level. If he went up it lived with him; if he dropped it was alongside of him. It was quaint to see the other guns correcting their range, but always a bit after the fair. Of course, I knew it was Tam and I somehow knew he was just circling round trying out the new gun. How he escaped, the Lord knows!"

Faithful to his promise, Tam returned.

"If any of you gentlemen have a seegair—"he asked.

Half a dozen were offered to him and he took them all.

"A'll no' offend any o' ye," he explained, "by refusin' your hospitality. They mayn't be good seegairs, as A've reason to know, but A'll smoke them all in the spirit they are geeven."

He sat down on a big packing-case, tucked up his legs under him and pulled silently at the glowing Perfecto. Then he began:

"At eleven o'clock in the forenoon," said Tam, settling himself to the agreeable task, "in or about the vicinity of La Bas a solitary airman micht ha' been sighted or viewed, wingin' his way leisurely across the fleckless blue o' the skies. Had ye been near enough ye would have obsairved a smile that played aroond his gay young face. In his blue eyes was a look o' deep thought. Was he thinkin' of home, of his humble cot in the shadow of Ben Lomond? He was not, for he never had a home in the shadow of Ben Lomond. Was he thinkin' sadly of the meanness o' his superior officer who had left one common seegair in his box and had said, 'Tam, go into my quarters and help yourself to the smokes'?"

"Tam, I left twenty," said an indignant voice, "and when I came to look for them they were all gone."

"A've no doot there's a bad character amongst ye," said Tam gravely; "A' only found three, and two of 'em were bad, or it may have been four. No, sir- rs, he was no' thinkin' of airthly things. Suddenly as he zoomed to the heavens there was a loud crack; and lookin' over, the young hero discovered that life was indeed a bed of shrapnel and that more was on its way, for at every point of the compass Archie was belching forth death and destruction"—he paused and rubbed his chin—"Archie A' didn't mind," he said with a little chuckle, "but Archie's little sister, sir-r, she was fierce! She never left me. A' stalled an' looped, A' stood on ma head and sat on ma tail. A' banked to the left and to the right. A' spiraled up and A' nose-dived doon, and she stayed wi' me closer than a sister. For hoors, it seemed almost an etairnity, Tam o' the Scoots hovered with impunity above the inferno—

"But why, Tam?" asked Blackie. "Was it sheer swank on your part?"

"It was no swank," said Tam quietly. "Listen, Captain Blackie, sir-r; four guns were bangin' and bangin' at me, and one of them was a good one —too good to live. Suppose A' had spotted that one—A' could have dropped and bombed him."

Blackie was frowning.

"I think we'll leave the Archies alone," he said; "you have never shown a disposition to go gunning for Archies before, Tam."

Tam shook his head.

"It is a theery A' have, sir-r," he said; "yon Archie, the new feller, is being tried oot. He is different to the rest. Mr. Austin had him the other night. Mr. Colebeck was nearly brought doon yesterday morn. Every one in the squadron has had a taste of him, and every one in the squadron has been lucky."

"That is a fact," said Austin; "this new gun is a terror."

"But he has no' hit any one," insisted Tam; "it's luck that he has no', but it's the sort of luck that the flyin'-man has. To-morrow the luck may be all the other way, and he'll bring doon every one he aims at. Ma idea is that to-morrow we've got to get him, because if he makes good, in a month's time you won't be able to fly except at saxteen thoosand feet."

A light broke in on Blackie.

"I see, Tam," he said; "so you were just hanging around to discourage him?"

"A' thocht it oot," said Tam. "A' pictured ma young friend William von Archie shootin' and shootin', surroonded by technical expairts with long whiskers and spectacles. 'It's a rotten gun you've got, Von,' says they; 'can ye no' bring doon one wee airman?' 'Gi' me anither thoosand shots,' gasps Willie, 'and there'll be a vacant seat in the sergeant's mess;' and so the afternoon wears away and the landscape is littered wi' shell cases, but high in the air, glitterin' in the dyin' rays of the sun, sits the debonair scoot, cool, resolute, and death-defyin'."

That night the wires between the squadron headquarters and G. H. Q. hummed with information and inquiry. A hundred aerodromes, from the North Sea to the Vosges, reported laconically that Annie, the vicious sister of Archie, was unknown.

Tam lay in his bunk that night devouring the latest of his literary acquisitions.

Tam's "bunk" was a ten-by-eight structure lined with varnished pine. The furniture consisted of a plain canvas bed, a large black box, a home-made cupboard and three book-shelves which ran the width of the wall facing the door. These were filled with thin, paper-covered "volumes" luridly colored. Each of these issues consisted of thirty-two pages of indifferent print, and since the authors aimed at a maximum effect with an economy of effort, there were whole pages devoted to dialogue of a staccato character.

He lay fully dressed upon the bed. A thick curtain retained the light which came from an electric bulb above his head and his mind was absorbed with the breathless adventures of his cowboy hero.

Now and again he would drop the book to his chest and gaze reflectively at the ceiling, for, all the time he had been reading, one-half of his brain had been steadily pursuing a separate course of inquiry of its own; and while the other half had wandered pleasantly through deep and sunless gulches or had clambered on the back of a surefooted bronco up precipitous mountain-slopes, the mental picture he conjured was in the nature of a double exposure, for ever there loomed a dim figure of a mysterious anti-aircraft gun. He took up the book for about the tenth time and read two lines, when a bell in the corner of the room rang three times. Three short thrills of sound and then silence.

Tam slipped from the bed, lifted down his leather jacket from the wall and struggled into it. He took up his padded helmet, switched off the light and, opening the door, stepped out into the darkness. Buttoning his jacket as he went, he made his way across by a short cut to the hangars and found Blackie surrounded by half a dozen officers already on the spot.

"Is that you, Tam? I want you to go up—there she goes!"

They listened.

"Whoom!"

"Fritz has sneaked across in the dark and is industriously bombing billets," he said; "he dodged the Creeper's Patrol. Go and see if you can find him."

"Whoom!"

The sound of the bursting bomb was nearer.

"'Tis safer in the air," said Tam as he swung into his fuselage. "Contact!"

A few seconds later, with a roar, the machine disappeared into the black wall of darkness.

It came back in less than a minute well overhead and Blackie, straining his eyes upward, followed its progress against the stars until it melted into the sky.

"Whoom!"

"He is looking for us," said Blackie; "stand by your hangars."

To the northwest two swift beams of light were sweeping the sky urgently. From a point farther south sprang another beam.

"If Fritz doesn't locate us now he ought to be shot," growled Blackie.

But apparently Fritz had overshot the aerodrome, for the next explosion came a mile to the west.

"Tam will see the burst," said young Austin and Blackie nodded.

There were no other explosions and they waited for ten minutes, then—

"Ticka-ticka-ticka-ticka!"

The sound came from right overhead.

"Tam's got him," whooped Blackie; "the devil must have been flying low."

"Tocka-tocka-tocka-tocka!"

"That's Fritz," said Blackie, "and that's Tam again."

Then one of the waving searchlights strayed in their direction, and down its white beam for the space of a hundred yards slid a ghostly white moth. It dipped suddenly and fell out of the light and in its wake, but above, burst three little green balls of fire—Tam's totem and sign-manual.

"Landing lights!" roared Blackie, and they had hardly been switched on when Tam swooped to the ground.

In the meantime a motor-car had gone swiftly in the direction of the fallen Hun machine.

"He crashed," said Tam breathlessly, as he jumped to the ground; "A'm afeered the puir body is hurt."

But the poor body was neither hurt nor frightened, nor indeed had he crashed.

In point of fact he had made a very good landing, considering the disadvantages under which he labored. They brought him into the mess-room, a tall stripling with shaven head and blue laughing eyes, and he took the coffee they offered him with a courteous little bow and a click of his heels.

"Baron von Treutzer," the prisoner introduced himself.

"I was afraid that a thousand meters was too low to fly, even at night," he said; "I suppose I didn't by any lucky chance get you. By the way, who brought me down? Tam?"

"Tam it was," said Blackie cheerfully, "and you didn't get us."

"I am sorry," said the baron. "May I ask you whether it was Tam who was doing stunts over our new gun?"

Blackie nodded.

"I thought it was. They have been cursing him all the evening —I mean, of course, the technical people," he added hastily, as though to emphasize the fact that the Imperial Air Service was above resentment. "Naturally they swore you had some kind of armor on your machine, and though we told them it was most unlikely, they insisted—you know what obstinate people these manufacturers are; in fact, they say that they saw it glitter," he laughed softly. "You see," he went on, "they don't understand this game. They can not understand why their wonderful"—he corrected himself swiftly —"why their gun did not get you. It would have been a terrible disappointment if they had brought you down and discovered that you were not sheeted in some new patent shell-proof steel."

"Oh, aye," said Tam, and he smiled, which was an unusual thing for Tam to do, and then he laughed, a deep, bubbling chuckle of laughter, which was even more unusual. "Oh, aye," he said again and was still laughing when he went out of the little anteroom.

He did not go back to his bunk, but made his way to the workshop, and when he went up the next morning he carried with him, carefully strapped to the fuselage, a sheet of tin which he had industriously cut and punched full of rivet-holes in the course of the night.

"And what are you going to do with that, Tam?" asked Blackie.

"That is ma new armor," said Tam solemnly. "'Tis a grand invention I made out of my own head."

"But what is the idea?" asked Blackie.

"Captain Blackie, sir-r," said Tam, "I have a theery, and if you have no objection I'd like to try it oot."

"Go ahead," said Blackie with a perplexed frown.

At half-past eleven, Tam, having roved along the German front-line trenches and having amused himself by chasing a German spotter to earth, made what appeared to be a leisurely way back to that point of the Lille road where he had met with his adventures of the previous day. He was hoping to find the battery which he had worried at that time, and he was not disappointed. In the same area where he had met the guns before, they opened upon him. He circled round and located six pieces. Which of these was "Annie"?

One he could silence at terrible risk to himself, but no more. To drop down, on the off-chance of finding his quarry, was taking a gambler's chance, and Tam prided himself that he was no gambler. That the gun was there, he knew. Its shells were bursting ever upon his level and he was bumped and kicked by the violence of the concussions. As for the other guns, he ignored them; but from whence came the danger? He had unstrapped the tin-plate and held it ready in his gloved hand—then there came a burst dangerously near. He banked over, side-slipped in the most natural manner and with all his strength flung the tin-plate clear of the machine. Immediately after, he began to climb upward. He looked down, catching the glitter of the tin as it planed and swooped to the earth.

He knew that those on the ground below thought he was hit. For a brief space of time the guns ceased firing and by the time they recommenced they fired short. Tam was now swooping round eastward farther and farther from range, and all the time he was climbing, till, at the end of half an hour, those who watched him saw only a little black speck in the sky.

When he reached his elevation he began to circle back till he came above the guns and a little to the eastward. He was watching now intently. He had located the six by certain landmarks, and his eyes flickered from one point to the other. A drifting wisp of cloud helped him a little in the period of waiting. It served the purpose of concealment and he passed another quarter of an hour dodging eastward and westward from cover to cover until, heading back again to the west, he saw what he had been waiting for.

Down charged the nose of the machine. Like a hawk dropping upon its prey he swooped down at one hundred and fifty miles an hour, his eyes fixed upon one point. The guns did not see him until too late. Away to his right, two Archies crashed and missed him by the length of a street. He slowly flattened before he came over a gun which stood upon a big motor-trolley screened by canvas and reeds, and he was not fifty yards from the ground when he released, with almost one motion, every bomb he carried.

The explosion flung him up and tossed his little machine as though it were of paper. He gave one fleeting glance backward and saw the débris, caught a photographic glimpse of half a dozen motionless figures in the road, then set his roaring machine upward and homeward.

It was not until a week afterward that the news leaked out that Herr Heinzelle, one of Krupp's best designers, had been "killed on the Western Front," and that information put the finishing touch to Tam's joy.

"But," asked the brigadier-general to whose attention Tam's act of genius had been brought, "how did your man know it was the gun?"

"You see, sir," said Blackie, "Tam got to know that Fritz believed his machine was armored, and he thought they would be keen to see the armor, and so he took up a plate of tin and dropped it. What was more natural than that they should retrieve the armor and take it to the experts for examination? Tam waited till he saw the sunlight reflected on the tin near one of the guns —knew that he had found his objective—and dropped for it!"

"An exceedingly ingenious idea!" said the brigadier.

This message Blackie conveyed to his subordinate.

"A'm no' puffed-up aboot it," said Tam. "'Twas a great waste o' good tin."

CHAPTER VI

THE LAW-BREAKER AND FRIGHTFULNESS

It is an unwritten law of all flying services that when an enemy machine bursts into flames in the course of an aerial combat the aggressor who has brought the catastrophe should leave well enough alone and allow his stricken enemy to fall unmolested.

Lieutenant Callendar, returning from a great and enjoyable strafe, was met by three fast scouts of the Imperial German Flying Service. He shot down one, when his gun was jammed. He banked over and dived to avoid the attentions of the foremost of his adversaries, but was hit by a chance bullet, his petrol tank was pierced and he suddenly found himself in the midst of noisy flames which said "Hoo-oo-oo!"

As he fell, to his amazement and wrath, one of his adversaries dropped after him, his machine-gun going like a rattle. High above the combatants a fourth and fifth machine, the one British and the other a unit of the American squadron, were tearing down-skies. The pursuing plane saw his danger, banked round and sped for home, his companion being already on the way.

"Ye're no gentleman," said Tam grimly, "an' A'm goin' to strafe ye!"

Fortunately for the flying breaker of air-laws, von Bissing's circus was performing stately measures in the heavens and as von Bissing's circus consisted of ten very fast flying-machines, Tam decided that this was not the moment for vengeance and came round on a hairpin turn just as von Bissing signaled, "Attack!"

Tam got back to the aerodrome to discover that Callendar, somewhat burnt but immensely cheerful, was holding an indignation meeting, the subject under discussion being "The Game and How It Should Be Played."

"The brute knew jolly well I was crashing. It's a monstrous thing!"

"One was bound to meet fellows like that sooner or later," said Captain Blackie, the squadron commander, philosophically. "I suppose the supply of gentlemen does not go round, and they are getting some rubbish into the corps. One of you fellows drop a note over their aerodrome and ask them what the dickens they mean by it. Did you see him, Tam?"

"A' did that," said Tam; "that wee Hoon was saved from destruction owing to circumstances ower which A' had no control. A' was on his tail; ma bricht- blue eyes were glancin' along the sichts of ma seelver-plated Lewis gun, when A' speered the grand circus of Mr. MacBissing waiting to perform."

Tam shook his head.

"A'm hoping," said he, "that it was an act of mental aberration, that 'twas his first crash; and, carried away by the excitement and enthusiasm of the moment, the little feller fell into sin. A'm hoping that retribution is awaiting him.

"'Ma wee Hindenburg,' says Mr. MacBissing, stern and ruthless, 'did I no see ye behavin' in a manner likely to bring discredit upon the Imperial and All-Highest Air Sairvice of our Exalted and Talkative Kaiser? Hoch! Hoch! Hoch!'

"Little Willie Hindenburg hangs his heid.

"'Baron,' or 'ma lord,' as the case may be, says he, 'I'll no be tellin' ye a lie. I was not mesel'! That last wee dram of sauerkraut got me all lit up like a picture palace!' says he; 'I didn't know whether it was on ma heid or somebody else's,' says he; 'I'll admit the allegation and I throw mesel' on the maircy o' the court.'

"'Hand me ma strop,' says MacBissing, pale but determined, and a few minutes later a passer-by micht have been arrested and even condemned to death by hearin' the sad and witchlike moans that came frae headquarters."

That "Little Willie Hindenburg" had not acted inadvertently, but that it was part of his gentle plan to strafe the strafed—an operation equivalent to kicking a man when he is down—was demonstrated the next morning, for when Thornton fell out of control, blazing from engine to tail, a German flying-man, unmistakably the same as had disgraced himself on the previous day, came down on his tail, keeping a hail of bullets directed at the fuselage, though he might have saved himself the trouble, for both Thornton and Freeman, his observer, had long since fought their last fight.

Again Tam was a witness and again, like a raging tempest, he swept down upon the law-breaker and again was foiled by the vigilant German scouts from executing his vengeance.

Tam had recently received from home a goodly batch of that literature which was his peculiar joy. He sat in his bunk on the night of his second adventure with the bad-mannered airman, turned the lurid cover of "The Seven Warnings: The Story of a Cowboy's Vengeance," and settled himself down to that "good, long read" which was his chiefest and, indeed, his only recreation. He began reading at the little pine table. He continued curled up in the big armchair—retrieved from the attic of the shell-battered Château d'Enghien. He concluded the great work sitting cross-legged on his bed, and the very restlessness which the story provoked was a sure sign of its gripping interest.

And when he had finished the little work of thirty-two pages, he turned back and read parts all over again, a terrific compliment to the shy and retiring author. He closed the book with a long sigh, sat upon his bed for half an hour and then went back to the pine table, took out from the débris of one of the drawers a bottle of ink, a pen and some notepaper and wrote laboriously and carefully, ending the seven or eight lines of writing with a very respectable representation of a skull and cross-bones.

When he had finished, he drew an envelope toward him and sat looking at it for five minutes. He scratched his head and he scratched his chin and laid down his pen.

It was eleven o'clock, and the mess would still be sitting engaged in discussion. He put out the light and made his way across the darkened aerodrome.

Blackie saw him in the anteroom, for Tam enjoyed the privilege of entrée at all times.

"His name? It's very curious you should ask that question, Tam," smiled Blackie; "we've just had a message through from Intelligence. One of his squadron has been brought down by the Creepers, and they are so sick about him that this fellow who was caught by the Creepers gave him away. His name is von Mahl, the son of a very rich pal of the Kaiser, and a real bad egg."

"Von Mahl," repeated Tam slowly, "and he will be belongin' to the Roulers lot, A'm thinkin'?"

Blackie nodded.

"They complain bitterly that he is not a gentleman," he said, "and they would kick him out but for the fact that he has this influence. Why did you want to know?"

"Sir-r," said Tam solemnly, "I ha'e a grand stunt."

He went back to his room and addressed the envelope:

"Mr. von Mahl."

The next morning when the well-born members of the Ninety- fifth Squadron of the Imperial German Air Service were making their final preparations to ascend, a black speck appeared in the sky.

Captain Karl von Zeiglemann fixed the speck with his Zeiss glasses and swore.

"That is an English machine," he said; "those Bavarian swine have let him through. Take cover!"

The group in the aerodrome scattered.

The Archie fire grew more and more furious and the sky was flecked with the smoke of bursting shell, but the little visitor came slowly and inexorably onward. Then came three resounding crashes as the bombs dropped. One got the corner of a hangar and demolished it. Another burst into the open and did no damage, but the third fell plumb between two machines waiting to go up and left them tangled and burning.

The German squadron-leader saw the machine bank over and saw, too, something that was fluttering down slowly to the earth. He called his orderly.

"There's a parachute falling outside Fritz. Go and get it."

He turned to his second in command.

"We shall find, Müller, that this visitor is not wholly unconnected with our dear friend von Mahl."

"I wish von Mahl had been under that bomb," grumbled his subordinate. "Can't we do something to get rid of him, Herr Captain?"

Zeiglemann shook his head.

"I have suggested it and had a rap over the knuckles for my pains. The fellow is getting us a very bad name."

Five minutes later his orderly came to the group of which Zeiglemann was the center and handed him a small linen parachute and a weighted bag. The squadron-leader was cutting the string which bound the mouth of the bag when a shrill voice said:

"Herr Captain, do be careful; there might be a bomb."

There was a little chuckle of laughter from the group, and Zeiglemann glowered at the speaker, a tall, unprepossessing youth whose face was red with excitement.

"Herr von Mahl," he snapped with true Prussian ferocity, "the air- services do not descend to such tricks nor do they shoot at burning machines."

"Herr Captain," spluttered the youth, "I do what I think is my duty to my Kaiser and my Fatherland."

He saluted religiously.

To this there was no reply, as he well knew, and Captain Zeiglemann finished his work in silence. The bag was opened. He put in his hand and took out a letter.

"I thought so," he said, looking at the address; "this is for you, von Mahl." He handed it to the youth, who tore open the envelope.

They crowded about him and read it over his shoulder:

"THIS IS THE FIRST WARNING OF THE AVENGER.
SHAKE IN YEER SHOES. TREMBLE!
Surround ye'sel' with guards and walls
And hide behind the cannon balls,
And dig ye'sel' into the earth.
Ye'll yet regret yeer day of birth.
For Tam the Scoot is on yeer track
And soon yeer dome will start to crack!"

It was signed with a skull and cross-bones.

The young man looked bewildered from one to the other. Every face was straight.

"What—what is this?" he stammered; "is it not absurd? Is it not frivolous, Herr Captain?"

He laughed his high, shrill little laugh, but nobody uttered a sound.

"This is serious, of course, von Mahl," said Zeiglemann soberly. "Although this is your private quarrel, the squadron will do its best to save you."

"But, but this is stupid foolishness," said von Mahl as he savagely tore the note into little pieces and flung them down. "I will go after this fellow and kill him. I will deal with this Herr Tam."

"You will do as you wish, Herr von Mahl, but first you shall pick up those pieces of paper, for it is my order that the aerodrome shall be kept clean."

Tam swooped back to his headquarters in time for breakfast and made his report.

"The next time you do tricks over Roulers they'll be waiting for you, Tam," said Blackie with a shake of his head. "I shouldn't strain that warning stunt of yours."

"Sir-r," said Tam, "A've no intention of riskin' government property."

"I'm not thinking of the machine, but of you."

"A' was thinkin' the same way," said Tam coolly. "'Twould be a national calamity. A' doot but even the Scotsman would be thrown into mournin' —'Intelligence reaches us,' says our great contempor'y, 'from the Western Front which will bring sorrow to nearly every Scottish home reached by our widely sairculated journal, an' even to others. Tam the Scoot, the intreepid airman, has gone west. The wee hero tackled single-handed thairty- five enemy 'busses, to wit, Mr. MacBissing's saircus, an' fell, a victim to his own indomitable fury an' hot temper, after destroyin' thairty-one of the enemy. Glascae papers (if there are any) please copy.'"

That Blackie's fears were well founded was proved later in the morning. Tam found the way to Roulers barred by an Archie barrage which it would have been folly to challenge. He turned south, avoiding certain cloud masses, and had the gratification of seeing "the circus" swoop down from the fleece in a well-designed encircling formation.

Tam swung round and made for Ypres, but again found a barring formation.

He turned again, this time straight for home, dropping his post-bag (he had correctly addressed his letter and he knew it would be delivered), shot down out of control a diving enemy machine that showed fight, chased a slow "spotter" to earth, and flashed over the British trenches less than two hundred feet from the ground with his wings shot to ribbons—for the circus had got to within machine-gun range.

A week later Lieutenant von Mahl crossed the British lines at a height of fifteen hundred feet, bombed a billet and a casualty clearing station and dropped an insolent note addressed to "The Englishman Tamm." He did not wait for an answer, which came at one o'clock on the following morning—a noisy and a terrifying answer.

"This has ceased to be amusing," said Captain von Zeiglemann, emerging from his bomb-proof shelter, and wired a requisition for three machines to replace those "destroyed by enemy action," and approval for certain measures of reprisal. "As for that pig-dog von Mahl..."

"He has received his fifth warning," said his unsmiling junior, "and he is not happy."

Von Mahl was decidedly not happy. His commandant found him rather pale and shaking, sitting in his room. He leaped up as von Zeiglemann entered, clicked his heels and saluted. Without a word the commandant took the letter from his hand and read:

If ye go to Germany A'll follow ye. If ye gae hame to yeer mither A'll find the house and bomb ye. A'll never leave ye, McMahl. — TAM THE AVENGER.

"So!" was von Zeiglemann's comment.

"It is rascality! It is monstrous!" squeaked the lieutenant. "It is against the rules of war! What shall I do, Herr Captain?"

"Go up and find Tam and shoot him," said Zeiglemann dryly. "It is a simple matter."

"But—but—do you think—do you believe—?"

Zeiglemann nodded.

"I think he will keep his word. Do not forget, Herr Lieutenant, that Tam brought down von Müller, the greatest airman that the Fatherland ever knew."

"Von Müller!"

The young man's face went a shade paler. The story of von Müller and his feud with an "English" airman and of the disastrous sequel to that feud, was common knowledge throughout Germany.

Walking back to Command Headquarters, von Zeiglemann expressed his private views to his confidant.

"If Tam can scare this money-bag back to Frankfurt, he will render us a service."

"He asked me where I thought he would be safe—he is thinking of asking for a transfer to the eastern front," said Zeiglemann's assistant.

"And you said—"

"I told him that the only safe place was a British prison camp."

"Please the good God he reaches there," said Zeiglemann piously, "but he will be a fortunate man if he ever lands alive from a fight with Tam. Do not, I command you, allow him to go up alone. We must guard the swine— keep him in the formation."

Von Zeiglemann went up in his roaring little single-seater and ranged the air behind the German lines, seeking Tam. By sheer luck he was brought down by a chance Archie shell and fell with a sprained ankle in the German support-trenches, facing Armentiers.

"A warning to me to leave Mahl to fight his own quarrels," he said as he limped from the car which had been sent to bring him in.

There comes to every man to whom has been interpreted the meaning of fear a moment of exquisite doubt in his own courage, a bewildering collapse of faith that begins in uneasy fears and ends in blind panic.

Von Mahl had courage—an airman can not be denied that quality whatever his nationality may be—but it was a mechanical valor based upon an honest belief in the superiority of the average German over all — friends or rivals.

He had come to the flying service from the Corps of the Guard; to the Corps of the Guard from the atmosphere of High Finance, wherein men reduce all values to the denomination of the mark and appraise all virtues by the currency of the country in which that virtue is found.

His supreme confidence in the mark evaporated under the iron rule of a colonel who owned three lakes and a range of mountains and an adjutant who had four surnames and used them all at once.

His confidence in the superiority of German arms, somewhat shaken at Verdun, revived after his introduction to the flying service, attained to its zenith at the moment when he incurred the prejudices of Tam, and from that moment steadily declined.

The deterioration of morale in a soldier is a difficult process to reduce to description. It may be said that it has its beginnings in respect for your enemy and reaches its culminating point in contempt for your comrades. Before you reach that point you have passed well beyond the stage when you had any belief in yourself.

Von Mahl had arrived at the level of descent when he detached himself from his comrades and sat brooding, his knuckles to his teeth, reviewing his abilities and counting over all the acts of injustice to which he had been subjected.

Von Zeiglemann, watching him, ordered him fourteen days' leave, and the young officer accepted the privilege somewhat reluctantly.

There was a dear fascination in the danger, he imagined. He had twice crossed fire with Tam and now knew him, his machine, and his tactics almost intimately.

Von Mahl left for Brussels en route for Frankfurt and two days later occurred one of those odd accidents of war which have so often been witnessed.

Tam was detailed to make one of a strong raiding party which had as its objective a town just over the Belgian-German frontier. It was carried out successfully and the party was on its way home when Tam, who was one of the fighting escort, was violently engaged by two machines, both of which he forced down. In the course of a combat he was compelled to come to within a thousand feet of the ground and was on the point of climbing when, immediately beneath him, a long military railway train emerged from a tunnel. Tam carried no bombs, but he had two excellent machine guns, and he swooped joyously to the fray.

A few feet from the ground he flattened and, running in the opposite direction to that which the train was taking, he loosed a torrent of fire into the side of the carriages.

Von Mahl, looking from the window of a first-class carriage, saw in a flash the machine and its pilot—then the windows splintered to a thousand pieces and he dropped white and palpitating to the floor.

He came to Frankfurt to find his relations had gone to Karlsruhe, and followed them. The night he arrived Karlsruhe was bombed by a French squadron... von Mahl saw only a score of flying and vengeful Tams. He came back to the front broken in spirit and courage. "The only place you can be safe is an English internment camp."

He chewed his knuckles with fierce intentness and thought the matter over.

"A'm delayin' ma seventh warnin'," said Tam, "for A'm no' so sure that McMahl is aboot. A've no' seen the wee chiel for a gay lang time."

"Honestly, Tam," said young Craig (the last of the Craigs, his two brothers having been shot down over Lille), "do you really think you scare Fritz?"

Tam pulled at his cigar with a pained expression, removed the Corona from his mouth, eyeing it with a disappointed sneer, and sniffed disparagingly before he replied.

"Sir-r," he said, "the habits of the Hoon, or Gairman, ha'e been ma life study. Often in the nicht when ye gentlemen at the mess are smokin' bad seegairs an' playin' the gamblin' game o' bridge-whist, Tam o' the Scoots is workin' oot problems in Gairman psych—I forget the bonnie waird. There he sits, the wee man wi'oot so much as a seegair to keep him company — thank ye, sir-r, A'll not smoke it the noo, but 'twill be welcomed by one of the sufferin' mechanics—there sits Tam, gettin' into the mind, or substitute, of the Hoon."

"But do you seriously believe that you have scared him?"

Tam's eyes twinkled.

"Mr. Craig, sir-r, what do ye fear wairst in the world?"

Craig thought a moment.

"Snakes," he said.

"An' if ye wanted to strafe a feller as bad as ye could, would ye put him amongst snakes?"

"I can't imagine anything more horrible," shuddered Craig.

"'Tis the same with the Hoon. He goes in for frichtfulness because he's afraid of frichtfulness. He bombs little toons because he's scairt of his ain little toons bein' bombed. He believes we get the wind up because he'd be silly wi' terror if we did the same thing to him. Ye can always scare a Hoon — that's ma theery, sir-r."

Craig had no further opportunity for discussing the matter, for the next morning he was "concussed" in midair and retained sufficient sense to bring his machine to the ground. Unfortunately the ground was in the temporary occupation of the German.

So Craig went philosophically into bondage.

He was taken to German Headquarters and handed over to von Zeiglemann's wing "for transport."

"This is Mr. von Mahl," introduced Zeiglemann gravely (they were going in to lunch); "you have heard of him."

Craig raised his eyebrows, for the spirit of mischief was on him.

"Von Mahl," he said with well-assumed incredulity; "why, I thought —oh, by the way, is to-day the sixteenth?"

"To-morrow is the sixteenth," snarled von Mahl. "What happens to-morrow, Herr Englishman?"

"I beg your pardon," said Craig politely; "I'm afraid I can not tell you —it would not be fair to Tam."

And von Mahl went out in a sweat of fear.

From somewhere overhead came a sound like a snarl of a buzz- saw as it bites into hard wood. Tam, who was walking along a deserted by-road, his hands in his breeches pockets, his forage cap at the back of his head, looked up and shaded his eyes. Something as big as a house-fly, and black as that, was moving with painful slowness across the skies.

Now, there is only one machine that makes a noise like a buzz-saw going about its lawful business, and that is a British battle-plane, and that this was such a machine, Tam knew.

Why it should be flying at that height and in a direction opposite to that in which the battle-line lay, was a mystery.

Usually a machine begins to drop as it reaches our lines, even though its destination may be far beyond the aerodromes immediately behind the line —even, as in this case, when it was heading straight for the sea and the English coast. Nor was it customary for an aeroplane bound for "Blighty" to begin its voyage from some point behind the German lines. Tam stood for fully five minutes watching the leisurely speck winging westward; then he retraced his steps to the aerodrome.

He found at the entrance a little group of officers who were equally interested.

"What do you make of that bus, Tam?" asked Blackie.

"She's British," said Tam cautiously.

He reached out his hands for the glasses that Blackie was offering, and focused them on the disappearing machine. Long and silently he watched her. The sun had been behind a cloud, but now one ray caught the aeroplane for a moment and turned her into a sparkling star of light. Tam put down his glasses.

"Yon's Mr. Craig's," he said impressively.

"Craig's machine? What makes you think so?"

"Sir-r," said Tam, "I wad know her anywheer. Yon's Mr. Craig's 'bus, right enough."

Blackie turned quickly and ran to his office. He spun the handle of the telephone and gave a number.

"That you, Calais? There's a Boche flying one of our machines gone in your direction—yes, one that came down in his lines last week. A Fairlight battle-plane. She's flying at sixteen thousand feet. Warn Dover."

He hung up the telephone and turned back.

Holiday-makers at a certain British coast town were treated to the spectacle of an alarm.

They gathered on the sands and on the front and watched a dozen English machines trekking upward in wide circles until they also were hovering specks in the sky. They saw them wheel suddenly and pass out to sea and then those who possessed strong glasses noted a new speck coming from the east and presently thirteen machines were mixed up and confused, like the spots that come before the eyes of some one afflicted with a liver.

From this pickle of dots one slowly descended and the trained observers standing at a point of vantage whooped for joy, for that which seemed a slow descent was, in reality, moving twice as fast as the swiftest express train and, moreover, they knew by certain signs that it was falling in flames.

A gray destroyer, its three stacks belching black smoke, cut through the sea and circled about the débris of the burning machine. A little boat danced through the waves and a young man was hauled from the wreckage uttering strange and bitter words of hate.

They took him down to the ward-room of the destroyer and propped him in the commander's armchair. A businesslike doctor dabbed two ugly cuts in his head with iodine and deftly encircled his brow with a bandage. A navigating lieutenant passed him a whisky-and-soda.

"If you speak English, my gentle lad," said the commander, "honor us with your rank, title, and official number."

"Von Mahl," snapped the young man, "Royal Prussian Lieutenant of the Guard."

"You take our breath away," said the commander. "Will you explain why you were flying a British machine carrying the Allied marks?"

"I shall explain nothing," boomed the youth.

He was not pleasant to look upon, for his head was closely shaven and his forehead receded. Not to be outdone in modesty, his chin was also of a retiring character.

"Before I hand you over to the wild men of the Royal Naval Air Service, who, I understand, eat little things like you on toast, would you like to make any statement which will save you from the ignominious end which awaits all enterprising young heroes who come camouflaging as enterprising young Britons?"

Von Mahl hesitated.

"I came—because I saw the machine—it had fallen in our lines—it was an impulse."

He slipped his hand into his closely buttoned tunic and withdrew a thick wad of canvas-backed paper which, unfolded, revealed itself as a staff map of England.

This he spread on the ward-room table and the commander observed that at certain places little red circles had been drawn.

"Uppingleigh, Colnburn, Exchester," said the destroyer captain; "but these aren't places of military importance—they are German internment camps."

"Exactly!" said von Mahl; "that is where I go."

In this he spoke the truth, for to one of these he went.

CHAPTER VII

THE MAN BEHIND THE CIRCUS

There comes to every great artist a moment when a sense of the futility of his efforts weighs upon and well-nigh crushes him. Such an oppression represents the reaction which follows or precedes much excellent work. The psychologist will, perhaps, fail to explain why this sense of emptiness so often comes before a man's best accomplishments, and what association there is between that dark hour of anguish which goes before the dawn of vision, and the perfect opportunity which invariably follows.

Sergeant-Pilot Tam struck a bad patch of luck. In the first place, he had missed a splendid chance of catching von Rheinhoff, who with thirty-one "crashes" to his credit came flaunting his immoral triumph in Tam's territory. Tam had the advantage of position and had attacked—and his guns had jammed. The luck was not altogether against him, for, if every man had his due, von Rheinhoff should have added Tam's scalp to the list of his thirty-one victims.

Tam only saved himself by taking the risk of a spinning nose dive into that zone of comparative safety which is represented by the distance between the trajectories of high-angle guns and the flatter curve made by the flight of the eighteen-pounder shell.

Nor were his troubles at an end that day, for later he received instructions to watch an observation balloon, which had been the recipient of certain embarrassing attentions from enemy aircraft. And in some miraculous fashion, though he was in an advantageous position to attack any daring intruder, he had been circumvented by a low-flying Fokker.

The first hint he received that the observation balloon was in difficulties came when he saw the two observers leap into space with their parachutes, and a tiny spiral of smoke ascend from the fat and helpless "sausage."

Tam dived for the pirate machine firing both guns—then, for the second time that day, the mechanism of his gun went wrong.

"Accidents will happen," said the philosophical Blackie; "you can't have it all your own way, Tam. If I were you I'd take a couple of days off — you can have ten days' leave if you like, you're entitled to it."

But Tam shook his head. "A'll tak' a day, sir-r," he said, "for meditation an' devotional exercise wi' that wee bit gun."

So he turned into the workshop and stripped the weapon, calling each part by name until he found, in a slovenly fitted ejector, reason and excuse for exercising his limitless vocabulary upon that faithless part. He also said many things about the workman who had fitted it.

"Angus Jones! O Angus Jones!" said Tam, shaking his head.

Tam never spoke of anybody impersonally. They were christened instantly and became such individual realities that you could almost swear that you knew them, for Tam would carefully equip them with features and color, height and build, and frequently invented for the most unpopular of his imaginary people relatives of offensive reputations.

"Angus, ma wee lad," he murmured as his nimble fingers grew busy, "ye've been drinkin' again! Nay, don't deny it! A' see ye comin' out of Hennessy's the forenoon. An' ye've a wife an' six children, the shame on ye to treat a puir woman so! Another blunder like this an' ye'll lose yeer job."

A further fault was discovered in a stiff feed-block, and here Tam grew bitter and personal.

"Will ye do this, Hector Brodie McKay? Man, can ye meet the innocent gaze o' the passin' soldiery an' no' feel a mairderer? An' wi' a face like that, ravaged an' seaun fra' vicious livin'—for shame, ye scrimshankin', lazy guid-for-nawthing!"

He worked far into the night, for he was tireless, and appeared on parade the next morning fresh and bright of eye.

"Tam, when you're feeling better I'd like you to dodge over the German lines. Behind Lille there's a new Hun Corps Headquarters, and there's something unusual on."

Tam went out that afternoon in the clear cold sky and found that there was indeed something doing.

Lille was guarded as he had never remembered its being guarded before, by three belts of fighting machines. His first attempt to break through brought a veritable swarm of hornets about his ears. The air reverberated with Archie fire of a peculiar and unusual intensity long before he came within striking distance of the first zone.

Tam saw the angry rush of the guardian machines and turned his little Nieuport homeward.

"A'richt! A'richt! What's frichtenin' ye?" he demanded indignantly, as they streaked behind his tail. "A'm no' anxious to put ma nose where it's no' wanted!"

He shook off his pursuers and turned on a wide circle, crossed the enemy's line on the Vimy Ridge and came back across the black coal-fields near Billy-Montigny. But his attempt to run the gauntlet and to cross Lille from the eastward met with no better success, and he escaped via Menin and the Ypres salient.

"Ma luck's oot," he reported glumly. "There's no road into Lille or ower Lille—ye'd better send a submarine up the Liza."

Tam had never thoroughly learned the difference between the Yser and the Lys and gave both rivers a generic title.

"Did you see any concentrations east of the town?" asked Blackie.

"Beyond an epidemic of mad Gairman airplanes an' a violent eruption of Archies, the hatefu' enemy shows no sign o' life or movement," said Tam. "Man, A've never wanted so badly to look into Lille till now."

Undoubtedly there was something to hide. Young Turpin, venturing where Tam had nearly trod, was shot down by gun-fire and taken prisoner. Missel, a good flyer, was outfought by three opponents and slid home with a dead observer, limp and smiling in the fuselage.

"To-morrow at daybreak, look for Tam amongst the stars," said that worthy young man as he backed out of Blackie's office, "the disgustin' incivility o' the Hoon has aroosed the fichtin' spirit o' the dead-an'-gone MacTavishes. Every fiber in ma body, includin' ma suspenders, is tense wi' rage an' horror."

"A cigar, Tam?"

"No, thank ye, sir-r," said Tam, waving aside the proffered case and extracting two cigars in one motion. "Well, perhaps A'd better. A've run oot o' seegairs, an' the thoosand A' ordered frae ma Glasgae factor hae been sunk by enemy action—this is no' a bad seegair, Captain Blackie, sir-r. It's a verra passable smoke an' no' dear at four-pence."

"That cigar costs eight pounds a hundred," said Blackie, nettled.

"Ye'll end yeer days in the puirhouse," said Tam.

True to his promise he swept over Lille the next morning and to his amazement no particular resistance was offered. He was challenged half- heartedly by a solitary machine, he was banged at by A-A guns, but encountered nothing of that intensity of fire which met him on his earlier visit.

And Lille was the Lille he knew: the three crooked boulevards, the jumble of small streets, and open space before the railway station. There was no evidence of any unusual happening—no extraordinary collection of rolling stock in the tangled sidings, or gatherings of troops in the outskirts of the town.

Tam was puzzled and pushed eastward. He pursued his investigations as far as Roubaix, then swept southward to Douai. Here he came against exactly the same kind of resistance which he had found on his first visit to Lille. There were the three circles of fighting machines, the strengthened Archie batteries, the same furious eagerness to attack.

Tam went home followed by three swift fighters. He led them to within gliding distance of the Allied lines; then he turned, and this time his guns served him, for he crashed one and forced one down. The third went home and told Fritz all about it.

"It's verra curious," said Tam, and Blackie agreed.

Tam went out again the following morning—but this time not alone. Six fighting machines, with Blackie leading, headed for Douai in battle formation. At Douai they met no resistance—the aerial concentration had vanished and, save for the conventional defenses, there was nothing to prevent their appearance over the town. That same afternoon Captain Sutton, R.F.C., looking for an interest in life over Menin, found it. He came back with his fuselage shot to chips and wet through from a smashed radiator.

"So far as I can discover," he said, "all the circuses are hovering about Menin. Von Bissing's is there and von Rheinhoff's, and I could almost swear I saw von Wentzl's red scouts."

"Did you get over the town?"

Sutton laughed. "I was a happy man when I reached our lines," he said.

"Maybe they're trying out some new stunt," said Blackie. "Probably it is a plan of defense—a sort of divisional training—I'll send a report to G. H. Q. I don't like this concentration of circuses in our neighborhood."

Now a "circus" is a strong squadron of German airplanes attached to no particular army, but employed on those sectors where its activities will be of most value at a critical time; and its appearance is invariably a cause for rejoicing among all red-blooded adventurers.

Two days after Blackie had made his report, von Bissing's World-Renowned Circus was giving a performance, and on this occasion was under royal and imperial patronage.

For, drawn up by the side of the snowy road, some miles in the rear of the line were six big motor-cars, and on a high bank near to the road was a small group of staff officers muffled from chin to heels in long gray overcoats, clumsily belted at the waist.

Aloof from the group was a man of medium height, stoutly built and worn of face, whose expression was one of eager impatience. The face, caricatured a hundred thousand times, was hawklike, the eyes bright and searching, the chin out-thrust. He had a nervous trick of jerking his head sideways as though he were everlastingly suffering from a crick in the neck.

Now and again he raised his glasses to watch the leader as he controlled the evolutions of the twenty-five airplanes which constituted the "circus."

It was a sight well worth watching.

First in a great V, like a flock of wild geese, the squadron swept across the sky, every machine in its station. Then, at a signal from the leader, the V broke into three diamond-shaped formations, with the leader at the apex of the triangle which the three flights formed. Another signal and the circus broke into momentary confusion, to reform with much banking and wheeling into a straight line—again with the leader ahead. Backward and forward swept the line; changed direction and wheeled until the machines formed a perfect circle in the sky.

"Splendid!" barked the man with the jerking head.

An officer, who stood a few paces to his rear, stepped up smartly, saluted, and came rigidly to attention.

"Splendid!" said the other again. "You will tell Captain Baron von Bissing that I am pleased and that I intend bestowing upon him the Order Pour la Mérite. His arrangements for my protection at Lille and Douai and Menin were perfect."

"Majesty," said the officer, "your message shall be delivered."

The sightseer swept the heavens again. "I presume that the other machine is posted as a sentinel," he said. "That is a most excellent idea— it is flying at an enormous height. Who is the pilot?"

The officer turned and beckoned one of the group behind him. "His Majesty wishes to know who is the pilot of the sentinel machine?" he asked.

The officer addressed raised his face to the heavens with a little frown.

"The other machine, general?" he repeated. "There is no other machine."

He focused his glasses on the tiniest black spot in the skies. Long and seriously he viewed the lonely watcher, then:

"General," he said hastily, "it is advisable that his Majesty should go."

"Huh?"

"I can not distinguish the machine, but it looks suspicious."

"Whoom! Whoom!"

A field away, two great brown geysers of earth leaped up into the air and two deafening explosions set the bare branches of the trees swaying.

Down the bank scrambled the distinguished party and in a few seconds the cars were streaking homeward.

The circus was now climbing desperately, but the watcher on high had a big margin of safety.

"Whoom!"

Just to the rear of the last staff car fell the bomb, blowing a great hole in the paved road and scattering stones and débris over a wide area.

The cars fled onward, skidding at every turn of the road, and the bombs followed or preceded them, or else flung up the earth to left or right.

"That's the tenth and the last, thank God!" said the sweating aide-de- camp. "Heaven and thunder! what an almost catastrophe!"

In the amazing spaces of the air, a lean face, pinched and blue with the cold, peered over the fuselage and watched the antlike procession of pin- point dots moving slowly along the snowy road.

"That's ma last!" he said, and picking up an aerial torpedo from between his feet, he dropped it over the side.

It struck the last car, which dissolved noisily into dust and splinters, while the force of the explosion overturned the car ahead.

"A bonnie shot," said Tam o' the Scoots complacently, and banked over as he turned for home. He shot a glance at the climbing circus and judged that there was no permanent advantage to be secured from an engagement. Nevertheless he loosed a drum of ammunition at the highest machine and grinned when he saw two rips appear in the wing of his machine.

By the time he passed over the German line all the Archies in the world were blazing at him, but Tam was at an almost record height—the height where men go dizzy and sick and suffer from internal bleeding. Over the German front-line trenches he dipped steeply down, but such had been his altitude that he was still ten thousand feet high when he leveled out above his aerodrome.

He descended in wide circles, his machine canted all the time at an angle of forty-five degrees and lighted gently on the even surface of the field a quarter of an hour after he had crossed the line.

He descended to the ground stiff and numb, and Bertram walked across from his own machine to make inquiries.

"Parky, Tam?"

"It's no' so parky, Mr. Bertram, sir-r," replied Tam cautiously.

"Rot, Tam!" said that youthful officer. "Why, your nose is blue!"

"Aweel," admitted Tam. "But that's no' cold, that's—will ye look at ma altitude record?"

The young man climbed into the fuselage, looked and gasped.

"Dear lad!" he said, "have you been to heaven?"

"Verra near, sir-r," said Tam gravely; "another ten gallons o' essence an' A'd 'a' made it. A've been that high that A' could see the sun risin' to- morrow!"

He started to walk off to his quarters but stopped and turned back. "Don't go near MacBissing's caircus," he warned; "he's feelin' sore."

Tam made a verbal report to Blackie, and Blackie got on to Headquarters by 'phone.

"Tam seems to have had an adventure, sir," he said, when he had induced H. Q. exchange to connect him with his general and gave the lurid details.

"It might be Hindenburg," said the general thoughtfully. "He's on the Western Front somewhere—that may explain the appearance of the circuses —or it may have been a corps general showing off the circus to a few trippers from Berlin—they are always running Reichstag members and pressmen round this front. Get Tam to make a report—his own report, not one you have edited." Blackie heard him chuckle. "I showed the last one to the army commander and he was tickled to death—hurry it along, I'm dying to see it."

If there is one task which an airman dislikes more than any other, it is report-writing. Tam was no exception, and his written accounts of the day's work were models of briefness.

In the days of his extreme youth he had been engaged in labor which did not call for the clerical qualities, and roughly his written "reports" were modeled on the "time sheets" he was wont to render in that far-off period, when he dwelt in lodgings at Govan, and worked at McArdle's Shipbuilding Yard.

Thus:

Left aerodrome 6 A. M. Enemy patrols encountered 5 Ditto ditto chased 4 Ditto ditto forced down 2 Bombs dropped on Verleur Station 5 etc., etc.

Fortunately Tam possessed a romantic and a poetical soul, and there were rare occasions when he would offer a lyrical account of his adventures containing more color and detail. As, for example, his account of his fight with Lieutenant Prince Zwartz-Hamelyn:

"Oh, wad some power the giftie gi'e us Tae see oursel's as ithers see us." Thus spake a high an' princely Hun As he fired at Tam wi' his Maxim gun. Thinkin', na doot, that bonnie lad Was lookin', if no' feelin', bad. But Tam he stalled his wee machine An' strafft young Zwartz-Hamelyn.

It was Blackie who harnessed Tam's genius for description to the pencil of a stenographer, and thereafter, when a long report was needed by Headquarters, there would appear at Tam's quarters one Corporal Alexander Brown, Blackie's secretary, and an amiable cockney who wrote mystic characters in a notebook with great rapidity.

"Is it ye, Alec?" said Tam, suspending his ablutions to open the door of his "bunk." "Come away in, man. Is it a report ye want? Sit down on the bed an' help yeersel' to the seegairs. Ye'll find the whisky in the decanter."

Corporal Brown sat on the bed because he knew it was there. He dived into his pocket and produced a notebook, a pencil and a cigaret, because he knew they had existence, too. He did not attempt to search for the cigars and the whisky because he had been fooled before, and had on two separate occasions searched the bunk for these delicacies under the unsmiling eyes of Tam and aided by Tam's advice, only to find in the end that Tam was as anxious to discover such treasures as the baffled corporal himself.

"We will noo proceed with the thrillin' serial," said Tam, spreading his towel on the window-ledge and rolling down his shirt-sleeves. "Are ye ready, Alec?"

"'Arf a mo', Sergeant—have you got a match?"

"Man, ye're a cadger of the most appallin' descreeption," said Tam severely. "A'm lookin' for'ard to the day when it'll be a coort-martial offense to ask yeer superior officer for matches—here's one. Don't strike it till ye give me one of yeer common cigarets."

The corporal produced a packet.

"A'll ask ye as a favor not to let the men know A've descended to this low an' vulgar habit," said Tam. "A'll take two or three as curiosities — A'd like to show the officers the kind o' poison the lower classes smoke—"

"Here! Leave me a couple!" said the alarmed non-commissioned officer as Tam's skilful fingers half emptied the box.

"Be silent!" said Tam, "ye're interruptin' ma train o' thochts— what did A' say last?"

"You said nothing yet," replied the corporal, rescuing his depleted store.

"Here it begins," said Tam, and started:

"At ten o'clock in the forenoon o' a clear but wintry day, a solitary airman micht hae been seen wingin' his lane way ameedst the solitude o' the achin' skies."

"'Achin' skies'?" queried the stenographer dubiously.

"It's poetry," said Tam. "A' got it oot o' a bit by Roodyard Kiplin', the Burns o' England, an' don't interrupt.

"He seemed ower young for sich an adventure—"

"How old are you, Sergeant, if I may ask the question?" demanded the amanuensis.

"Ye may not ask, but A'll tell you—A'm seventy-four come Michaelmas, an' A've never looked into the bricht ees o' a lassie since A' lost me wee Jean, who flit wi' a colonel o' dragoons, in the year the battle of Balaklava was fought—will ye shut yeer face whilst A'm dictatin'?"

"Sorry," murmured the corporal and poised his pencil.

"Suddenly, as the wee hero was guidin' his 'bus through the maze o' cloods, a strange sicht met his ees. It was the caircus of MacBissing! They were evolutin' by numbers, performin' their Great Feat of Balancin' an' Barebacked Ridin', Aerial Trapeze an' Tight-rope Walkin', Loopin' the Loop by the death-defyin' Brothers Fritz, together with many laughable an' amusin' interludes by Whimsical Walker, the Laird o' Laughter, the whole concludin' with a Ground Patriotic Procession entitled Deutschland ower All—or Nearly All."

"I ain't seen a circus for years," said the corporal with a sigh. "Lord! I used to love them girls in short skirts—"

"Restrain yeer amorous thochts, Alec," warned Tam, "an' fix yeer mind on leeterature. To proceed:

"'Can it be,' says our hero, 'can it be that Mr. MacBissing is doin' his stunts at ten-thairty o' the clock in the cauld morn, for sheer love o' his seenister profession? No,' says A'—says our young hero— 'no,' says he, 'he has a distinguished audience as like as not.'

"Speerin' ower the side an' fixin' his expensive glasses on the groon, he espied sax motor-cars—"

The door was flung open and Blackie came in hurriedly. "Tam— get up," he said briefly. "All the damn circuses are out on a strafe— and we're It—von Bissing, von Rheinhoff, and von Wentzl. They're coming straight here and I think they're out for blood."

The history of that great aerial combat has been graphically told by the special correspondents. Von Bissing's formation—dead out of luck that day—was broken up by Archie fire and forced back, von Wentzl was engaged by the Fifty-ninth Squadron (providentially up in strength for a strafe of their own) and turned back, but the von Rheinhoff group reached its objective before the machines were more than five thousand feet from the ground and there was some wild bombing.

Von Rheinhoff might have unloaded his bombs and got away, but he showed deplorable judgment. To insure an absolutely successful outcome to the attack he ordered his machines to descend. Before he could recover altitude the swift little scouts were up and into the formation. The air crackled with the sound of Lewis-gun fire, machines reeled and staggered like drunken men, Tam's fighting Morane dipped and dived, climbed and swerved in a wild bacchanalian dance. Airplanes, British and German alike, fell flaming to the earth before the second in command of the enemy squadron signaled, "Retire."

A mile away a battery of A-A guns waited, its commander's eyes glued to a telescope.

"They're breaking off—stand by! Range 4300 yards— deflection—There they go! Commence firing."

A dozen batteries were waiting the signal. The air was filled with the shriek of speeding shells, the skies were mottled with patches of smoke, white and brown, where the charges burst.

Von Rheinhoff's battered squadron rode raggedly to safety.

"Got him—whoop!" yelled a thousand voices, as from one machine there came a scatter of pieces as a high-explosive shell burst under the wing, and the soaring bird collapsed and came trembling, slowly, head-over-heels to the ground.

Von Rheinhoff, that redoubtable man, was half conscious when they pulled him out of the burnt and bloody wreck.

He looked round sleepily at the group about him and asked in the voice of a very tired man:

"Which—of—you—fellows—bombed— our Kaiser?"

Tam leant forward, his face blazing with excitement.

"Say that again, sir-r," he said.

Von Rheinhoff looked at him through half-opened eyes. "Tam— eh?" he whispered. "You—nearly put an empire—in mourning."

Tam drew a long breath, then turned away. "Nearly!" he said bitterly. "Did A' no' tell ye, Captain Blackie, sir-r, that ma luck was oot?"

CHAPTER VIII

A QUESTION OF RANK

Tam stood in the doorway of Squadron Headquarters and saluted.

"Come in, Sergeant Mactavish," said Blackie, and Tam's heart went down into his boots.

To be called by his surname was a happening which had only one significance. There was trouble of sorts, and Tam hated trouble.

"There are some facts which General Headquarters have asked me to verify —your age is twenty-seven?"

"Yes, sir-r."

"You hold the military medal, the French Médaille Militaire, the Russian medal of St. George and the French Croix de Guerre?"

"Oh, aye, Captain Blackie, sir-r, but A've no' worn 'em yet."

"You were created King's Corporal for an act of valor on January 17, 1915?" Blackie went on, consulting a paper.

"Yes, sir-r."

Blackie nodded. "That's all, Sergeant," he said, and as Tam saluted and turned, "oh, by-the-way, Sergeant—we had a brass ha—I mean a staff officer here the other day and he reported rather unfavorably upon a practise of yours—er—ours. It was a question of discipline —you know it is not usual for a non-commissioned officer to be on such friendly terms with—er—officers. And I think he saw you in the anteroom of the mess. So I told him something which was not at the time exactly true."

Tam nodded gravely.

For the first time since he had been a soldier he had a horrid feeling of chagrin, of disappointment, of something that rebuffed and hurt.

"A' see, sir-r," he said, "'tis no' ma wish to put mesel' forward, an' if A've been a wee bit free wi' the young laddies there was no disrespect in it. A' know ma place an' A'm no' ashamed o' it. There's a shipyard on the Clyde that's got ma name on its books as a fitter—that's ma job an' A'm proud o' it. If ye're thinkin', Captain Blackie, sir-r, that ma heid got big—"

"No, no, Tam," said Blackie hastily, "I'm just telling you—so that you'll understand things when they happen."

Tam saluted and walked away.

He passed Brandspeth and Walker-Giddons and responded to their flippant greetings with as stiff a salute as he was capable of offering. They stared after him in amazement.

"What's the matter with Tam?" they demanded simultaneously, one of the other.

Tam reached his room, closed and locked the door and sat down to unravel a confused situation.

He had grown up with the squadron and had insensibly drifted into a relationship which had no counterpart in any other branch of the service. He was "Tam," unique and indefinable. He had few intimates of his own rank, and little association with his juniors. The mechanics treated him as being in a class apart and respected him since the day when, to the prejudice of good order and military discipline, he had followed a homesick boy who had deserted, found him and hammered him until nostalgia would have been a welcome relief. All deserters are shot, and the youth having at first decided that death was preferable to a repetition of the thrashing he had received, changed his mind and was tearfully grateful.

Sitting on his bed, his head between his hands, pondering this remarkable change which had come to the attitude of his officers and friends, Tam was sensible (to his astonishment) of the extraordinary development his mentality had undergone. He had come to the army resentfully, a rabid socialist with a keen contempt for "the upper classes" which he had never concealed. The upper classes were people who wore high white collars, turned up the ends of their trousers and affected a monocle. They spoke a kind of drawling English and said, "By gad, dear old top—what perfectly beastly weathah!"

They did no work and lived on the sweat of labor. They patronized the workman or ignored his existence, and only came to Scotland to shoot and fish —whereon they assumed (with gillies and keepers of all kinds) the national dress which Scotsmen never wear.

That was the old conception, and Tam almost gasped as he realized how far he had traveled from his ancient faith. For all these boys he knew were of that class—most of them had an exaggerated accent and said, "By gad!" —but somehow he understood them and could see, beneath the externals, the fine and lovable qualities that were theirs. He had been taken into this strange and pleasant community and had felt—he did not exactly know what he had felt. All he did know was that a brass-hatted angel with red tabs on its collar stood at the gate of a little paradise of comradeship, and forbade further knowledge of its pleasant places.

He pursed his lips and got to his feet, sick with a sense of his loss. He was of the people, apart. He was a Clydeside worker and they were the quality. He told himself this and knew that he lied—he and they stood on grounds of equality; they were men doing men's work and risking their lives one for the other.

Tam whistled a dreary little tune, took down his cap and walked over to the workshops. There was a motorcycle which Brandspeth told him he could use, and after a moment's hesitation, Tam wheeled the machine to the yard. Then he remembered that he was in his working tunic, and since it was his intention to utilize this day's leave in visiting a town at the rear of the lines, he decided to return to his bunk and change into his "best."

He opened his box—but his best tunic was missing.

"Weel, weel!" said Tam, puzzled, and summoned his batman with a shrill whistle.

"To tell you the truth, Sergeant," said the man, "Mr. Walker-Giddons and the other young officers came over for it three days ago. They got me to give it to 'em and made me promise I wouldn't say anything about it."

Tam smiled quietly.

"All right, Angus," he nodded and went back to his cycle. He did not know the joke, but it was one which would probably come to an untimely end, in view of the disciplinary measures which headquarters were taking. This incident meant another little pang, but the freshness of the morning and the exhilaration of the ride—for motorcycling has thrills which aviation does not know—helped banish all thoughts of an unpleasant morning.

He reached his destination, made a few purchases, drank an agreeable cup of coffee and discovered that he had exhausted all the joys which the town held. He had intended amusing himself through the day and returning at night, but, even before the restaurants began to fill for lunch he was bored and irritable, and strapping his purchases to the back of the cycle he mounted the machine and began his homeward journey.

It was in the little village St. Anton (in reality a suburb of the town) that he met Adventure—Adventure so novel, so bewildering, that he felt that he had been singled out by fate for such an experience as had never before fallen to mortal man.

He met a girl. He met her violently, for she was speeding along a road behind the wheel of a small motor ambulance and it happened that the road in question ran at right angles to that which Tam was following.

Both saw the danger a few seconds before the collision occurred; both applied fierce brakes, but, nevertheless, Tam found himself on his hands and knees at the feet of the lady-driver, having taken a purler almost into her lap, despite the printed warning attached to this portion of the ambulance:

DRIVER AND ORDERLIES ONLY

"Oh, I do hope you aren't hurt," said the girl anxiously.

Tam picked himself up, dusted his hands and his knees and surveyed her severely.

She was rather small of stature and very pretty. A shrapnel helmet was set at a rakish angle over her golden-brown hair, and she wore the uniform of a Red Cross driver.

"It was my fault," she went on. "This is only a secondary road and yours is the main—I should have slowed but I guess I was thinking of things. I often do that."

She was obviously American and Tam's slow smile was free of malice.

"It's fine to think of things," he said, "especially when y're drivin' an ambulance—but it's a hairse ye ought to be drivin', Mistress, if ye want to gie yeer thochts a good airin'."

"I'm really sorry," said the girl penitently. "I'm afraid your cycle is smashed."

"Don't let it worry ye," said Tam calmly. "It's no' ma bike anyway; it belongs to one of the hatefu' governin' classes, an' A've nothin' to do but mak' guid the damage."

"Oh," said the girl blankly, then she suddenly went red.

"Of course," she began awkwardly, "as I was responsible—I can well afford—"

She halted lamely and Tam's eyes twinkled. "Maybe ye're the niece of Andrew Carnegie an' ye've had yeer monthly library allowance," he said gravely, "an' maybe ye could spare a few thousand dollars or cents—A've no' got the exact coinage in ma mind—to help a wee feller buy a new whizzer-wheel. A' take it kindly, but guid money makes bad frien's."

"I didn't intend offering you money," she said hurriedly, flushing deeper than ever, "let me pull the car up to the side of the road."

Tam examined his own battered machine in the meantime. The front wheel had buckled, but this was easily remedied, and by the time the girl had brought her car to rest in a field he had repaired all the important damage.

"I was going to stop somewhere about here for lunch," she said, producing a basket from under the seat; "in fact, I was thinking of lunch when — when—"

"A' nose-dived on to ye," said Tam, preparing to depart. "Weel, A'll be gettin' along. There's nothing A' can do for ye?"

"You can stay and lunch with me."

"A've haid ma dinner," said Tam hastily.

"What did you have?" she demanded.

"Roast beef an' rice pudding," said Tam glibly.

"I don't believe you—anyway I guess it won't hurt you to watch me eat."

Tam noticed that she took it for granted that he was lying, for she served him with a portion of her simple meal, and he accepted the situation without protest.

"I'm an American, you know," she said as they sat cross-legged on the grass. "I come from Jackson, Connecticut—you've heard of Jackson?"

"Oh, aye," he replied. "A'm frae Glascae."

"That's Scotland—I like the Scotch."

Tam blushed and choked.

"I came over last year to drive an ambulance in the American Ambulance Section, but they wouldn't have me, so I just went into the English Red Cross."

"British," corrected Tam.

"I shall say English if I like," she defied him.

"Weel," said Tam, "it's no' for me to check ye if ye won't be edicated."

She stared at him, then burst into a ringing laugh. "My! the Scotch people are funny—tell me about Scotland. Is it a wonderful country? Do you know about Bruce and Wallace and Rob Roy and all those people?"

"Oh, aye," said Tam cautiously, "by what A' read in the paper it's a gay fine country."

"And the red deer and glens and things—it must be lovely."

"A've seen graund pictures of a glen," admitted Tam, "but the red deer in Glascae air no' sae plentifu' as they used to be—A'm thinkin' the shipyard bummer hae scairt 'em away."

She shot a sharp glance at him, then, it seemed for the first time, noticed his stripes.

"Oh, you're a sergeant," she said. "I thought—I thought by your 'wings' you were an officer. I didn't know that sergeants—"

Tam smiled at her confusion and when he smiled there was an infinite sweetness in the action.

"Ye're right, Mistress. A'm a sairgeant, an' A' thocht a' the time ye were mistakin' me for an officer, an' A'd no' the heart to stop ye, for it's a verra lang time since A' spoke wi' a lady, an' it was verra, verra fine."

He rose slowly and walked to his cycle—she ran after him and laid her hand on his arm.

"I've been a low snob," she said frankly. "I beg your pardon— and you're not to go, because I wanted to ask you about a sergeant of your corps —you know the man that everybody is talking about. He bombed the Kaiser's staff the other day. You've heard about it, haven't you?"

Tam kept his eyes on the distant horizon.

"Oh, he's no sae much o' a fellow—a wee chap wi' an' awfu' conceit o' himsel'."

"Nonsense!" she scoffed, "why, Captain Blackie told me—"

Suddenly, she stepped back and gazed at him wide-eyed. "Why! You're Tam!"

Tam went red.

"Of course you're Tam—you never wear your medal ribbons, do you? You're called—"

"Mistress," said Tam as he saluted awkwardly and started to push his machine, "they ca' me 'sairgeant,' an' it's no' such a bad rank."

He left her standing with heightened color blaming herself bitterly for her gaucherie.

So it made that difference, too!

For some reason he did not feel hurt or unhappy. He was in his most philosophical mood when he reached his aerodrome. He had a cause for gratification in that she knew his name. Evidently, it was something to be a sergeant if by so being you stand out from the ruck of men. As to her name he had neither thought it opportune nor proper to advance inquiries.

He smiled as he changed into his working clothes and wondered why.

A dozen girl drivers were waiting on the broad road before the 131st General Hospital the next morning, exchanging views on the big things which were happening in their little world, when one spied an airplane.

"Gracious—isn't it high! I wonder if it's a German— they're bombing hospitals—it's British, silly—no, it's a German, I saw one just like that over Poperinghe—it's coming right over."

"Stand by your cars, ladies, please."

The tall "chief's" sharp voice scattered the groups.

"He's dropping something—it's a bomb—no, it's a message bag. Look at the streamers!"

A bag it was and when they raced to the field in which it fell they discovered that it was improvised, roughly sewn and weighted with sand.

The superintendent read the label and frowned.

"'To the Driver of Ambulance B. T. 9743, 131st General Hospital' — this is evidently for you, Miss Laramore."

"For me, Mrs. Crane?"

Vera Laramore came forward, a picture of astonishment and took the bag.

"Oh, what fun—who is it, Vera? Open it quickly."

The girl pulled open the bag and took out a letter. It bore the same address as that which had been written on the label.

Slowly she tore off the end of the envelope.

There was a single sheet of paper written in a boyish hand. Without any preliminary it ran:

"A sairgeant-pilot, feelin' sair,
A spitefu' thing may do,
An' so I come to you once mair
That I may say—an' true—
As you looked doon on me ane day,
Now I look doon on you!

"You, fra your height of pride an' clan
Heard your high spirit ca',
An' so you scorned the common man—
I saw yeer sweet face fa';
But, losh! I'm just that mighty high I can't see you at a'!"

It was signed "T" and the girl's eyes danced with joy. She shaded her eyes and looked up. The tiny airplane was turning and she waved her handkerchief frantically.

"A friend of yours?" asked the superintendent with ominous politeness.

"Ye-es—it's Tam, Mrs. Crane—I ran into him— he ran into me yesterday—"

"Tam?" even the severe superintendent was interested, "that remarkable man—I should like to see him. Everybody is talking about him just now. Was it a private letter or an official message from the aerodrome?"

"It was private," said the girl, very pink and a note of defiance in her voice, and the superintendent very wisely dropped the subject.

"I really don't know how to send him an appropriate answer," said Vera to her confidante and room-mate that evening. "I can't write poetry and I can't fly."

"I shouldn't answer it," said her sensible friend briskly. "After all, my dear, you don't want to start a flirtation with a sergeant—I mean, it's hardly the thing, is it?"

The little pajama'd figure sitting on the edge of the bed favored her friend with a cold stare.

"I certainly am not thinking of a flirtation," she said icily, "but if I were, I should as certainly be unaffected by the rank of my victim. In America we aren't quite so strong for pedigrees and families as you English people —"

"Irish," said the other gently.

Vera laughed as she curled up in the bed and drew her sheet up to her chin.

"It's queer how people hate being called English—even Tam—"

"Look here, Vera," said her companion hotly, "just leave that young man alone. And please get all those silly, romantic ideas out of your head."

A silence—then,

"I'm going to write to him, to-morrow," said a sleepy voice, and the rapid fire of her friend's protest was answered with a well-simulated snore.

Tam received the letter by messenger.

"Dear Mr. Tam (it ran):

I know that is your Christian name, but I really do not know your other, so will you please excuse me? I am going into Amiens next Friday and if you have quite forgiven me, will you please meet me for lunch at the Café St. Pierre? And thank you so much for your very clever verse."

"'Vera Laramore,'" repeated Tam. "A've no doot she's Scottish."

He trod air that week, literally and figuratively, for the work was heavy. The high winds which had kept the British squadrons to the ground, petered out to gentle breezes, and the air was alive with craft. Bombing raid, photographic reconnaissance and long-distance scouting kept the airmen busy. New squadrons appeared which had never been seen before on this front. The Franco-American unit came up from X, and did some very audible fraternizing with what was locally known as "Blackie's lot," a circumstance which ordinarily would have caused Tam's heart to rejoice.

But Tam was keeping clear of the mess-room just now, and he either sent an orderly with his messages or waited religiously on the mat. As for the officers, he avoided them unless (as was often the case) they sought him out.

Brandspeth brought one of the new men over to his bunk the night the American contingent arrived.

"I want you to meet an American officer, Tam," he yelled. "Don't be an ass—open the door."

He was on one side of the locked door and Tam was on the other.

Tam turned the key reluctantly and admitted the visitors.

"A'm no' wishin' to be unceevil, Mr. Brandspeth, but Captain Blackie will strafe ye if he finds ye here."

"Rubbish! I want you to meet Mr. Laramore."

Tam looked at the keen-faced young athlete and slowly extended his hand.

"I think you know my sister," said the smiling youth, "and certainly we all know you."

He gave the pilot a grip which would have crushed a hand of ordinary muscularity.

"A've run up against the young lady in ma travels," said Tam solemnly.

Laramore laughed. "I saw her for a moment to-day and she asked me to remind you of your appointment."

"An appointment—with a lady? Oh, Tam!" said the shocked Brandspeth, producing from his overcoat pocket a siphon of soda, a large flask of amber- brown liquid and a bundle of cigars, and setting them upon the table. "Really, Tam is always making the strangest acquaintances."

"He never met anybody stranger than Vera—or better," said Laramore, with a little laugh. "Vera, I suppose, is worth a million dollars. She is a citizen of a neutral country. She can have the bulliest time any girl could desire, and yet she elects to come to France, drive a car over abominable roads which are more often than not under shell-fire, and sleep in a leaky old shack for forty cents a day."

Brandspeth was filling the glasses.

"You're a neutral, too—say when—I suppose you're not exactly a pauper and yet you risk breaking your neck for ten francs per. Help yourself to a cigar, Tam—I said a cigar."

"Try one o' mine, sir-r," said Tam coolly, and produced a box of Perfectos from under his bed; "ye may take one apiece and it's fair to tell ye A've coonted them."

They spent a moderate but joyous evening, but Tam, standing in the doorway of his "bunk," watched the figures of his guests receding into the darkness with a sense of depression. He had no social ambitions, he had no desire to be anything other than the man he was. If he looked forward to his return to civil life at the war's end, he did so with equanimity, though that return meant a life in soiled overalls amid the hum and clang of a factory shop.

He had none of that divine discontent which is half the equipment of Scottish youth. Rather did he possess ambition's surest antidote in a mild and kindly cynicism which stripped endeavor of its illusions.

It was on the Wednesday night after he had written a polite little note to the One Hundred and Thirty-first General Hospital accepting the invitation to lunch and had received one of Blackie's tentative permits to take a day's leave (Tam called them "D. V. Passes") that the blow fell.

"Angus," said Tam to his batman, "while A'm bravin' the terrors of the foorth dimension in the morn—"

"Is that the new scoutin' machine, Sergeant?" demanded the interested batman.

"The foorth dimension, ma puir frien', is a tairm applied by philosophers of the Royal Flyin' Coop to the space between France an' heaven."

"Oh, you mean the hair!" said the disappointed servant.

"A' mean the hair," replied Tam gravely, "not the hair that stands up when yeer petrol tank goes dry nor the hare yeer poachin' ancestors stole from the laird o' the manor, but the hair ye breathe when ye're no' smokin'. An' while A'm away in the morn A' want ye to go to Mr. Brandspeth's servant an' get ma new tunic. A'm going to a pairty at Amiens on Friday, an' A'm no' anxious to be walkin' doon the palm court of the Café St. Pierre in ma auld tunic."

"Anyway," said the batman, busily brushing that same "auld" tunic, "you wouldn't be walkin' into the Café St. Pierre."

"And why not?"

"Because," said the batman triumphantly, "that's one of the cafés reserved for officers only."

There was a silence, then: "Are ye sure o' that, Angus?"

"Sure, Sergeant—I was in Amiens for three months."

Tam said nothing and presently began whistling softly.

He walked to his book-shelf, took down a thin, paper-covered volume and sank back on the bed.

"That will do, Angus," he said presently; "ca' me at five."

The barriers were up all around—they had been erected in the course of a short week. They penned him to his class, confined him to certain narrow roads from whence he might see all that was desirable but forbidden.

He was so silent the next morning, when he joined the big squadron that was assembling on the flying field, that Blackie did not know he was there.

"Where's Tam? Oh, here you are. You know your position in the formation? Right point to cover the right of the American bombing squad. Mr. Sutton before you and Mr. Benson behind. You will get turning signals from me. Altitude twelve thousand—that will be two thousand feet above the bombers —no need to tell you anything. The objective is Bapaume and Achiet junctions—"

Tam answered shortly and climbed into his fuselage.

The squadron went up in twos, the fighting machines first, the heavier bombing airplanes last. For twenty minutes they maneuvered for position, and presently the leader's machine spluttered little balls of colored lights and the squadron moved eastward—a great diamond-shaped flock, filling the air and the earth with a tremulous roar of sound.

They reached their objectives without effective opposition. First, the junction to the north of Bapaume, then the web of sidings at Achiet smoked and flamed under the heavy bombardment. Quick splashes of light where the bombs exploded, great columns of gray smoke mushrooming up to the sky, then feeble licks of flame growing in intensity of brightness where the incendiary bombs, taking hold of stores and hutments, advertised the success of the raid.

The squadron swung for home.

Tam with one eye for his leader and one for the possible dangers on his flank, was a mere automaton. There was no opportunity for displaying initiative—he was a cog in the wheel.

Suddenly a new signal glowed from the leading machine and Tam threw a quick glance left and right and began to climb. The other fighters were rising steeply, though not at such an angle that they could not see their leader, who was a little higher than they. Another signal and they flattened, and Tam saw all that he had guessed.

"Ma guidness!" said Tam, "the sky's stiff wi' 'busses!"

There must have been forty enemy machines between the squadron and home. So far as Tam could see there were eight separate formations and they were converging from three points of the compass.

The safety of the squadron depended upon the individual genius of the fighters. Tam swerved to the right and dipped to the attack, his machine- guns spraying his nearest opponent. Sutton, ahead of him, was already engaged, and he guessed that Benson, in his rear, had his hands full.

Tam's nearest opponent went down sideways, his second funked the encounter and careered wildly away to his left and immediately lost position to attack, for when two forces are approaching one another at eighty miles an hour, failure to seize the psychological moment for striking your blow leaves you in one minute exactly three miles to the rear of your opponent. The first shock was over in exactly thirty-five seconds, and beneath the spot where the squadron had passed seven machines were diving or circling earthward, the majority of these in flames.

The second shock came three minutes later and again the squadron triumphed.

Then Tam, looking down, saw one of the bombing machines turn out of the line, and at the same time Blackie signaled, "Cover stragglers."

The squadron was now well behind the British lines, but they were south of the aerodrome, having changed direction to meet the attacks. Tam with a little leap of heart recognized in the distance a familiar triangular field of unsullied snow, searched for and found the rectangular block of tiny huts which formed No. 131 General Hospital and turned out of the line with a wild sense of exhilaration.

"She'll no' see me eat," he said, "but she shall see a graund ficht."

The bomber was swerving and dipping like a helpless wild duck seeking to shake off the three hawks that were now hovering over her.

"Let you be Laramore's machine, O Lord!" prayed Tam, and he prayed with the assurance that his prayer was already answered.

He came at the leading German and for a second the two machines streamed nickel at one another. Tam felt the wind of the bullets and knew his machine was struck. Then his enemy crumpled and fell. He did not wait to investigate. The bomber was firing up at his nearest opponent when Tam took the third in enfilade and saw the pilot's head disappear behind the protective armoring.

He swung round and saw the bombing machine diving straight for the earth with the German scout on his tail. Tam followed in a dizzy drop. Three thousand feet from earth the bombing machine turned a complete somersault and Tam's heart leaped into his mouth.

He banked over to follow the pursuing German and in the brief space of time which intervened before his enemy could adjust his direction to cover pilot and gunner, Tam had both in line. His two guns trembled and flamed for four seconds and then the German dropped straight for earth and crashed in a flurry of smoke and flying débris.

Tam looked backward. The bomber had pancaked and was drifting to a landing; the squadron was out of sight. Tam glided to the broad field before the hospital.

"I knew it was you—I knew it was you!"

He looked down from the fuselage at the bright upturned face.

"Oh, aye, it was me," he admitted, "an' A'm mighty glad ye was lookin', for A' was throwin' stunts for ye."

He was on the ground now, loosening the collar of his leather jacket. He stepped clear of the obstructing planes of his machine and looked anxiously toward the gentle slopes of the ridge on which the bomber had landed.

"Thank the guid Lord," he said and sighed his relief.

He was making a careful inspection of his own machine preparatory to returning to the aerodrome when the girl came running across the field to say good-by.

"I can't tell you just how I feel—how grateful I am. My brother says you saved his life. He was in that other machine, you know."

"A' knew it," said Tam. "'Twas a graund adventure, like you read aboot in books—'twas ma low, theatrical mind that wanted it so. Good-by, young lady."

"Till to-morrow—don't forget you're lunching with me at the Café St. Pierre."

Tam smiled gravely. "A'm afraid ye'll have to postpone that lunch," he said, "till—"

"Till to-morrow," she interrupted firmly, and Tam flew back to the aerodrome without explaining.

He was feeling the reaction of the morning's thrill, and when he landed he had no answer to make to the congratulations which were poured upon him.

He made his way to his hut. His batman was cleaning a pair of boots and stood stiffly as Tam entered.

"That'll do, Angus, ye may go," he said, and then saw the folded coat upon his bed. "Ah, ye got it back, did ye—well, A'll no' be needin' it."

He picked up the coat and frowned.

"This is no' mine, Angus."

"Your tunic is in the box, sir—this is the one the officers had made for you. They wanted your other tunic for the measurements."

Tam looked at the man.

"Yon's an officer's tunic, Angus," he said; "an' why do ye say 'sir' to me?"

Angus beamed and saluted with a flourish.

"It's in General Orders this morning, sir—you've got a commission, an' Mr. Brandspeth says that the mess will be expectin' you to lunch at one- thirty."

Tam sat down on the bed, biting his lip.

"Get oot, Angus," he said huskily, "an'—stay you! Ye'll find a seegair in the box under the bed—an', Angus, A'm lunchin' oot to- morrow."

CHAPTER IX

A REPRISAL RAID

There are certain animals famous to every member of the British Expeditionary Force.

There is a Welsh regiment's goat which ate up the plan of attack issued by a brigadier-general, who bore a striking resemblance to somebody who was not Napoleon, thus saving the Welsh regiment from annihilation and reproach. There is the dog of the Middlesex regiment, who always bit staff-officers and was fourteen times condemned to death by elderly and irascible colonels, and fourteen times rescued by his devoted comrades. There is the Canadians' tame chicken, who sat waiting for nine-inch shells to fall, and then scratched over the ground they had disturbed; and there is last, but not least, that famous mascot of General Hospital One-Three-One, Hector O'Brien.

Hector O'Brien was born in the deeps of a Congo forest. Of his early life little is known, but as far as can be gathered, he made his way to France by way of Egypt and Gallipoli and was presented by a grateful patient to the nursing sisters and ambulance staff of One-Three-One, and by them was adopted with enthusiasm.

Hector O'Brien did precious little to earn either fame or notoriety until one memorable day. He used to sit in the surgery, before a large packing- case, wistfully watching the skies and scratching himself in an absent-minded manner. A chimpanzee may not cogitate very profoundly, and the statement that he is a deep thinker though an indifferent conversationalist has yet to be proved; but it is certain that Hector O'Brien was a student of medicine, and that he did, on this memorable day to which reference has been made, perambulate the wards of that hospital from bed to bed, feeling pulses and shaking his head in a sort of melancholy helplessness which brought joy to the heart of eight hundred patients, some hundred doctors, nurses and orderlies, and did not in any way disturb the melancholy principal medical officer, who was wholly unconscious of Hector's impertinent imitations.

Second-Lieutenant Tam, who was a frequent visitor at One-Three-One, had at an early stage struck up a friendship with Hector and had, I believe, taken him on patrol duty, Hector strapped tightly to the seat, holding with a grip of iron to the fuselage and chattering excitedly.

Thereafter, upon the little uniform jacket which Hector wore on state occasions was stitched the wings of a trained pilot. It is necessary to explain Hector's association with the R.F.C. in order that the significance of the subsequent adventure may be thoroughly appreciated.

Tam was "up" one day and on a particular mission. He looked down upon a big and irregular checker-board covered with numbers of mad white lines, which radiated from a white center and seemed to run frantically in all directions save one. Across that course, and running parallel beneath three of them was a straight silver thread. At the edge of his vision and beyond the place where the white lines ended abruptly, there were two irregular zigzags of yellow running roughly parallel. Behind each of these were thousands of little yellow splotches.

Tam banked over and came round on a hairpin turn, with his eyes searching the heavens above and below. A thousand feet beneath him was a straggling wisp of cloud, so tenuous that you saw the earth through its bulk. Above was a smaller cloud, not so transparent, but too thin to afford a lurking place for his enemy.

Tam was waiting for that famous gentleman, the "Sausage-Killer," the sworn foe of all "O. B.'s."

He paid little attention to the flaming lines because the "Sausage- Killer" never came direct from his aerodrome. You would see him streaking across the sky, apparently on his urgent way to the sea bases and oblivious of the existence of Observation Balloons.

Then he would turn, as though he had forgotten his passport and railway ticket and must go home quickly to get them. And before anybody realized what was happening, he would be diving straight down at the straining gas-bags, his tracer bullets would be ranging the line, and from every car would jump tiny black figures. You saw them falling straight as plummets till their parachutes took the air and opened. And there would be a great blazing and burning of balloons, frantic work at the winches which pulled them to earth, and the ballooning section would send messages to the aerodrome whose duty it was to protect them, apologizing for awakening the squadron from its beauty sleep, but begging to report that hostile aircraft had arrived, had performed its dirty work and had departed with apparent immunity.

The "Sausage-Killer" was due at 11.20, and at 11.18 Tam saw one solitary airplane sweep wide of the balloon park, and turn on a course which would bring him along the line of the O. B.'s. Apparently, the "Sausage-Killer" was not so blessed in the matter of sight as Tam, for the scout was on his tail and was pumping nickel through his tractor's screw before the destroyer of innocent gas-bags realized what had happened.

"It was a noble end," said Tam after he had landed, "and A'm no' so sure that he would have cared to be coonted oot in any other saircumstances; for the shepherd likes to die amongst his sheep and the captain on his bridge, and this puir feller was verra content, A've no doot, to crash under the een of his wee —"

"Did you kill him, Tam?" asked Blackie.

"A'm no' so sure he's deid in the corporeal sense," said Tam cautiously, "but he is removed from the roll of effectives."

So far from being dead, the "Sausage-Killer," who, appropriately enough, was ludicrously like a young butcher, with his red fat face and his cold blue eye, was very much alive and had a grievance.

"Where did that man drop from?" he demanded truculently, "I didn't see him."

"I'm sorry," said Blackie; "if we had known that, we would have got him to ring a bell or wave a flag."

"That is frivolous," said the German officer severely.

"It is the best we can do, dear lad," said Blackie, and didn't trouble to invite him to lunch.

"Tam, you've done so well," said the squadron leader at that meal, "that I can see you being appointed official guardian angel to the O. B.'s. They are going to bring you some flowers."

"And a testimonial with a purse of gold," suggested Croucher, the youngest of the flyers.

"A'm no' desirin' popularity," said Tam modestly, "'tis against ma principles to accept any other presents than seegairs, and even these A'm loath to accept unless they're good ones."

He looked at his wrist watch, folded his serviette and rose from the mess- table with a little nod to the president.

It was a gratifying fact, which Blackie had remarked, that Second Lieutenant, late Sergeant, Tam, had taken to the mess as naturally as a duck to water. He showed neither awkwardness nor shyness, but this was consonant with his habit of thought. Once attune your mind to the reception of the unexpected, so that even the great and vital facts of life and death leave you unshaken and unamazed, and the lesser quantities are adjusted with ease.

Tam had new quarters, his batman had become his servant, certain little comforts which were absent from the bunk were discoverable in the cozy little room he now occupied.

His day's work was finished and he was bound on an expedition which was one part business and nine parts joy-ride, frank and undisguised, for the squadron-car had been placed at his disposal. The road to Amiens was dry, the sun was up, and the sky was blue, and behind him was the satisfactory sense of good work well done, for the "Sausage-Killer" was at that moment on his way back to the base, sitting vis-à-vis with a grimy young military gentleman who cuddled a rifle and a fixed bayonet with one hand and played scales on a mouth-organ with the other, softly, since he was a mere learner, and this was an opportunity for making joyful noises without incurring the opprobrium of his superiors.

Tam enjoyed the beauty and freshness of the early afternoon, every minute of it. He drove slowly, his eyes wandering occasionally from the road to make a professional scrutiny of the skies. He spotted the lonely watches of 89 Squadron and smiled, for 89 had vowed many oaths that they would catch the "Sausage-Killer," and had even initiated a sweepstakes for the lucky man who crashed him.

At a certain quiet restaurant on the Grand' Place he found a girl waiting for him, a girl in soiled khaki, critically examining the menu.

She looked up with a smile as the young man came in, hung his cap upon a peg and drew out the chair opposite.

"I have ordered the tea, though it is awfully early," she said; "now tell me what you have been doing all the morning."

She spoke with an air of proprietorship, a tone which marked the progress of this strange friendship, which had indeed gone very far since Tam's violent introduction to Vera Laramore on the Amiens road.

"Weel," said Tam, and hesitated.

"Please don't give me a dry report," she warned him. "I want the real story, with all its proper fixings."

"Hoo shall A' start?" asked Tam.

"You start with the beginning of the day. Now, properly, Tam."

Her slim finger threatened him.

"Is it literature ye'd be wanting?" asked Tam shyly.

She nodded, and Tam shut his eyes and began after the style of an amateur elocutionist:

"The dawn broke fair and bonny an' the fairest rays of the rising sun fell upon the sleeping 'Sausage-Killer'—"

"Who is the 'Sausage-Killer'?" asked the girl, startled.

"He'll be the villain of the piece, A'm thinkin'," said Tam, "but if ye interrupt—"

"I am sorry," murmured the girl, apologetically.

She sat with her elbows on the table, her chin resting on her clasped hands and her eyes fixed on Tam, eyes that danced with amusement, with admiration, and with just that hint of tenderness that you might expect in the proud mother showing off the accomplishments of her first-born.

"—fell aboot the heid of the Sausage-Killer,'" Tam went on, "bathin' his shaven croon wi' saft radiance. There was a discreet tap at the door, and Wilhelm MacBethmann, his faithful retainer, staggered in, bearin' his cup of acorn coffee.

"'Rise, mein Herr,' says he, 'get oot o' bed, ma bonnie laird.'

"'What o'clock is it, Angus?' says the 'Sausage-Killer,' sitting up and rubbing his eyes.

"'It's seven, your Majesty,' says MacBethmann, 'shall I lay out yeer synthetic sausage or shall I fry up yesterday's sauerkraut?'

"But the 'Sausage-Killer' shakes his head.

"'Mon Angus,' he says, 'A've had a heedious dream. A' dreamt,' says he, 'that A' went for to kill a wee sausage and A' dived for him and missed him and before A' could recover, the sausage bit me. 'Tis a warning,' says he.

"'Sir,' says MacBethmann, trembling in every limb and even in his neck, 'ye'd be wise no' to go out the day.'

"But the prood 'Sausage-Killer' rises himself to his full length.

"'Unhand ma pants, Angus,' says he, 'ma duty calls,' and away goes the puir wee feller to meet his doom at the hands of the Terror of the Skies."

"That's you," said the girl.

"Ye're a good guesser," said Tam, pouring out the tea the waiter had brought. "Do ye take sugar or are ye a victim of the cocktail habit?"

"Did you kill him?" asked the girl.

"Poleetically and in a military sense the 'Sausage-Killer' is dead," said Tam; "as a human being he is still alive, being detained during his Majesty's displeasure."

"You will tell me the rest, won't you?" she pleaded. With her, Tam invariably ended his romances at the point where they could only be continued by the relation of his own prowess, "and I'm glad you brought him down — it makes me shudder to see the balloons burning. Oh, and do you know they bombed Number One-Three-One last night?"

"Ye don't say!"

There was amazement in his look, but there was pain, too. The traditions of the air service had become his traditions. A breach of the unwritten code by the enemy was almost as painful a matter to him as though it was committed by one of his own comrades. For his spiritual growth had dated from the hour of his enlistment, and that period of life wherein youth absorbs its most vivid and most eradicable impressions, had coincided with the two years he had spent in his new environment.

He understood nothing of the army and its intimate life, of its fierce and wholesome code. He could only wonder at the courage and the endurance of those men on the ground who were cheerful in all circumstances. They amazed and in a sense depressed him. He had been horrified to see snipers bayoneted without mercy, without being given a chance to surrender, not realizing that the sniper is outside all concession and can not claim any of the rough courtesies of war.

He had placed his enemy on a pedestal, and it hurt almost as much to know that the German fell short of his conception as it would have, had one of his own comrades been guilty of an unpermissible act.

Hospitals had been bombed before, but there was a chance that the wandering night-bird had dropped his pills in ignorance of what lay beneath him. Of late, however, hospitals and clearing stations had been attacked with such persistence that there was very little doubt that the enemy was deliberately carrying out a hideous plan.

"Ye don't say?" he repeated, and the girl noticed that his voice was a little husky. "Were ye—"he hesitated.

"I was on convoy duty, fortunately," said the girl, "but that doesn't save you in the daytime, and I have been bombed lots of times, although the red cross on the top of the ambulance is quite clear—isn't it?"

Tam nodded.

"There was no damage?" he asked anxiously.

"Not very much in one way," she said, "he missed the hospital but got the surgery and poor Hector—"She stopped, and he saw tears in her eyes.

"Ye don't tell me?" he asked, startled.

She nodded.

"Puir Hector; well, that's too bad, puir wee little feller!"

"Everybody is awfully upset about it, he was such a cheery little chap. He was killed quite—nastily." She hesitated to give the grisly details, but Tam, who had seen the effect of high explosive bombs, had no difficulty in reconstructing the scene where Hector laid down his life for his adopted country.

When he got back to the aerodrome that night he found that the bombing of hospitals was the subject which was exciting the mess to the exclusion of all others.

"It's positively ghastly that a decent lot of fellows like German airmen can do such diabolical things," said Blackie; "we are so helpless. We can't go along and bomb his collecting stations."

"Fritz's material is deteriorating," said a wing commander; "there's not enough gentlemen to go round. Everybody who knows Germany expected this to happen. You don't suppose fellows like Boltke or Immelmann or Richthoven would have done such a swinish thing?"

That same night One-Three-One was bombed again, this time with more disastrous effects. One of the raiders was brought down by Blackie himself, who shot both the pilot and the observer, but the raid was only one of many.

The news came through in the morning that a systematic bombing of field hospitals had been undertaken from Ypres to the Somme. At two o'clock that afternoon Blackie summoned his squadron.

"There's a retaliation stunt on to-night," he explained; "we are getting up a scratch raid into Germany. You fellows will be in for it. Tam, you will be my second in command."

At ten o'clock that night the squadron rose and headed eastward. The moon was at its full, but there was a heavy ground mist, and at six thousand feet a thin layer of clouds which afforded the raiders a little cover.

Tam was on the left of the diamond formation, flying a thousand feet above the bombers, and for an hour and a half his eyes were glued upon the signal light of his leader. Presently their objective came into sight: a spangle of lights on the ground. You could follow the streets and the circular sweep of the big Central Platz and even distinguish the bridges across the Rhine, then of a sudden the lights blurred and became indistinct, and Tam muttered an impatient "Tchk," for the squadron was running into a cloud-bank which might be small but was more likely to be fairly extensive.

They were still able to distinguish the locality, until three spurts of red flame in the very center of the town marked the falling of the first bombs. Then all the prominent lights went out. There were hundreds of feeble flickers from the houses, but after a while these too faded and died. In their place appeared the bright, staring faces of the searchlights as they swept the clouds.

Tam saw the flash of guns, saw the red flame-flowers of the bombs burst to life and die, and straining his eyes through the mist caught the "Return" signal of his leader. He banked round and ran into a thicker pall of fog and began climbing. As he turned he saw a quick, red, angry flash appear in the clouds and something whistled past his head. The guns had got the altitude of the bombers to a nicety and Tam grinned.

By this time Blackie's lights were out of sight and Tam was alone. He looked down at his compass and the quivering needle now pointed to his right, which meant he was on the homeward track. He kept what he thought was a straight course, but the needle swung round so that it pointed toward him. He banked over again to the right and swore as he saw the needle spin round as though some invisible finger was twirling it.

Now the airplane compass is subject to fits of madness.

There are dozens of explanations as to why such things occur, but the recollection of a few of these did not materially assist the scout. The thing to do was to get clear of the clouds and take his direction by the stars. He climbed and climbed, until his aeronometer pointed to twenty thousand feet. By this time it was necessary to employ the apparatus which he possessed for sustaining himself at this altitude. It was amazing that the clouds should be so high, and he began to think that his aeronometer was out of order when he suddenly dived up into the light of a cold moon.

He looked around, seeking the pole-star, and found it on his left. So all the time he had been running eastward.

And then his engine began to miss.

Tam was a philosopher and a philosopher never expects miracles. He understood his engine as a good jockey understands his horse. He pushed the nose of his machine earthward and planed down through an interminable bank of clouds until he found a gray countryside running up to meet him. There were no houses, no lights, nothing but a wide expanse of country dotted with sparse copses.

There was sufficient light to enable him to select a landing-place, and he came down in the middle of a big pasture on the edge of a forest of gaunt trees.

He unstrapped himself and climbed down, stretching his limbs before he took a gentle trot around the machine to restore his circulation. Then he climbed back into the fuselage and tinkered at the engine. He knew what was wrong and remedied the mischief in a quarter of an hour. Then he inspected his petrol supply and whistled. He had made a rough calculation and he knew within a few miles how far he was in the interior of Germany, and by the character of the country he knew he was in the marshy lands of Oosenburg, and there was scarcely enough petrol to reach the Rhine.

He left his machine, slipped an automatic pistol into the pocket of his overall and went on a voyage of exploration.

Half a mile from where he landed, he struck what he gathered was a high- road and proceeded cautiously, for the high-road would probably be patrolled, the more so if the noise of his machine had been correctly interpreted, though it was in his favor that he had shut off his engines and had planed down for five miles without a sound.

There was nobody in sight. To the left the road stretched in the diffused moonlight, a straight white ribbon unbroken by any habitation. To the right he discerned a small hut, and to this he walked. He had taken a dozen steps when a voice challenged him in German. At this point the road was sunken and it was from the shadow of the cutting that the challenge came.

"Hello," said Tam in English, and a little figure started out.

Tam saw the rifle in his hand and caught the glitter of a bayonet.

"You English?" said a voice.

"Scotch," said Tam severely.

"Aha!" There was a note of exultation. "You English-escaped prisoner! I haf you arrested and with me to the Commandant of Camp 74 you shall go."

"Is it English ye're speakin'?" said Tam.

The little man came closer to him. He stood four feet three and he was very fat. He wore no uniform, and was evidently one of those patriotic souls who undertake spare-time guard duty. His presence was explained by his greeting. Some men had escaped from the German prison-camp seven miles away and he was one of the sentries who were watching the road.

"You come mit me, vorwärts!"

Tam obeyed meekly and stepped out to the hut.

"I keep you here. Presently the Herr Leutnant will come and you shall go back."

He walked into the hut and waited in silence while the little man struck a match and lit an oil-lamp. The sentry fixed the glass chimney and turned to face the muzzle of Tam's automatic pistol.

"Sit down, ma wee frien'," said Tam; "let ma take that gun away from ye before ye hairt yeersel'—maircifu' Heavens!"

He was staring at the little man, but it was not the obvious terror of the civilian which fascinated him, it was the big, white, unshaven face, the long upper lip, and the low corrugated brow under the stiff-bristling hair, the small twinkling eyes, and the broad, almost animal, nose that held him for a moment speechless.

"Hector O'Brien!" gasped Tam, and almost lost his grasp of the situation in the discovery of this amazing likeness. "A' thought ye was dead," said Tam. "Oh, Hector, we have missed ye!"

The little man, his shaking hands uplifted, could only chatter incoherently. It needed this to complete the resemblance to the deceased mascot of One-Three-One.

"Ma puir wee man," said Tam, as he scientifically tied the hands of his prisoner, "so the Gairmans got ye after all."

"You shall suffer great punishment," his prisoner was spurred by fear to offer a protest. "Presently the Herr Leutnant will come with his motor-car."

"God bless ye for those encouraging words," said Tam. "Now will ye tell me how many soldiers are coming along?"

"Four—six—"began the prisoner.

"Make it ten," said Tam, examining the magazine of his pistol. "A' can manage wi' ten, but if there's eleven, A' shall have to fight 'im in a vulgar way wi' ma fists. Ye'll sit here," said he, "and ye will not speak."

He went to the untidy bed, and taking a coarse sacking-sheet he wound it about the man's mouth. Then he went to the door and waited.

Presently he heard the hum of the car, and saw two twinkling lights coming from the eastward. Nearer and nearer came the motor-car and pulled up with a jerk before the hut.

There were two men, a chauffeur and an officer, cloaked and overcoated, in the tonneau. The officer opened the door of the car and stepped down.

"Franz!" he barked. Tam stepped out into the moonlight.

"Is it ma frien' ye're calling?" he asked softly. "And will ye pit up yeer hands."

"Who—who—"demanded the officer.

"Dinna make a noise like an owl," said Tam, "or you will frighten the wee birdies. Get out of that, McClusky." This to the chauffeur.

He marched them inside the hut and searched them. The officer had come providentially equipped with a pair of handcuffs, which Tam used to fasten the well-born and the low-born together. Then he made an examination of the car, and to his joy discovered six cans of petrol, for in this deserted region where petrol stores are non-existent a patrol car carries two days' supply.

He brought his three prisoners out, loosened the bonds of the little man, and after a little persuasion succeeded in inducing his three unwilling porters to carry the tins across a rough field to where his plane was standing.

In what persiflage he indulged, what bitter and satirical things he said of Germans and Germany is not recorded. They stood in abject silence while he replenished his store of petrol and then—

"Up wi' ye," said he to Hector O'Brien's counterpart.

"For why?" asked the affrighted man.

"Up wi' ye," said Tam sternly; "climb into that seat and fix the belt around ye, quick—A'm taking ye back to yeer home!"

His pistol-point was very urgent and the little man scrambled up behind the pilot's seat.

"Now, you, McClusky," said Tam, following him and deftly strapping himself, "ye'll turn that propeller—pull it down so, d'ye hear me, ye miserable chauffeur!"

The man obeyed. He pulled over the propeller-blade twice, then jumped back as with a roar the engine started.

As the airplane began to move, first slowly and then gathering speed with every second, Tam saw the two men break into a run toward the road and the waiting motor-car.

Behind him he felt rather than heard slight grunts and groans from his unhappy passenger, and then at the edge of the field he brought up the elevator and the little scout, roaring like a thousand express trains, shot up through the mist and disappeared from the watchers on the road in the low-hanging clouds, bearing to the bereaved and saddened staff of One-Three-One Hector O'Brien's understudy.

CHAPTER X

THE LAST LOAD

Along a muddy road came an ambulance. It was moving slowly, zigzagging from side to side to avoid the shell holes and the subsidences which the collapse of ancient trenches on each side of the road had caused. It was a secondary or even a tertiary road, represented on the map by a spidery line, and was taken by driver Vera Laramore because there was no better.

From the rear end of the ambulance showed eight muddy soles, three pairs with toes upturned, the fourth at such an angle, one foot with the other, as to suggest a pain beyond any but this mute expression.

On the tail-board of the ambulance an orderly of the R. A. M. C. balanced himself, gaunt-eyed, unshaven, caked from head to foot in yellow mud, the red cross on his untidy brassard looming faintly from its grimy background. Beyond the soles with their worn and glaring nails, a disorderly rumple of brown army blankets, and between the stretchers a confusion of entangled haversacks, water-bottles and equipment, there was nothing to be seen of the patients, though a thin blue haze which curled along the tilt showed that one at least was well enough to smoke.

The ambulance made its slow way through the featureless country, past rubble heaps which had once been the habitations of men and women, splintered trunks of poplar avenues, great excavations where shells of an immense caliber had fallen long ago and the funnel shapes of which were now overgrown with winter weeds.

Presently the ambulance turned on to the main road and five people heaved a sigh of thankfulness, the sixth, he of the eloquent soles, being without interest in anything.

The car with its sad burden passed smoothly along the broad level road, such a road as had never been seen in France or in any other country before the war, increasing its speed as it went. Red-capped policemen at the crossroads held up the traffic—guns and mechanical transport, mud-splashed staff cars and tramping infantry edged closer to the side to let it pass.

Presently the car turned again, swept past a big aerodrome—the girl who drove threw one quick glance, had a glimpse of the parade-ground but did not recognize the man she hoped to see—and a few minutes later she was slowing the ambulance before the reception room of General Hospital One-Three-One.

The R. A. M. C. man dismounted, nodded to other R. A. M. C. men more tidy, more shaven, and a little envious it seemed of their comrade's dishabille and the four cases were lifted smoothly and swiftly and carried into the big hut.

"All right, driver," said the R. A. M. C. sergeant when four stretchers and eight neatly folded blankets had been put into the ambulance to replace those she had surrendered, and Vera, with a little jerk of her head, sent the car forward to the park.

She brought her machine in line with one of the four rows, checked her arrival and walked wearily over to her quarters. She had been out that morning since four, she had seen sights and heard sounds which a delicately nurtured young woman, who three years before had shuddered at the sight of a spider, could never in her wildest nightmare imagine would be brought to her sight or hearing. She was weary, body and soul, sick with the nausea which is incomparable to any other. And now she was at the end of it. Her application for long leave had followed the smashing up of her airman brother and his compulsory retirement in England.

And yet she could not bear the thought of leaving all this; the horror and the wonder of it were alike fascinating. She felt the same pangs of remorse she had experienced on the one occasion she had run away from school. She branded herself as a deserter and looked upon those who had the nerve and will to stay on with something of envy.

Her plain-spoken friend was sitting on her bed in a kimono as the girl came in.

"Well?" she asked.

"Well, what?" asked Vera irritably.

"Are you sorry you are leaving us?"

"I haven't left yet," said the girl, sitting down and unstrapping her leather leggings slowly.

"You don't go till to-morrow, that's true," said the other girl calmly, "and how have you rounded off all your little—friendships?" There was just the slightest of pauses between the two last words.

"You mean Lieutenant MacTavish?" asked Vera distraitly.

"I mean Tam," said the girl with a nod.

"Exactly what do you mean by 'rounded off'?"

The other girl laughed. "Well, there are many ways of a friendship," she smiled; "there's the 'If-you-come-to-my-town-look-me-up' way. There's the 'You'll-write-every-day' way—and—"She hesitated again.

"Go on," said Vera calmly.

"And there's—well, the conventional way."

Vera smiled. "I can't imagine Tam doing anything conventional," she said.

Elizabeth jumped up with a laugh, walked to the little bare dressing- table and began brushing her hair.

"Why do you laugh?" asked Vera.

"The whole thing's so curious," replied the girl. "Here's a man who is head-over-heels in love with you—"

"In love with me!"

Vera Laramore went red and white by turns and lost, for a moment, her grasp of the situation, then grew virtuously indignant, which was a tactical error for if she were innocent of such a thought as that which her friend expressed she should have been either amused or curious.

"How can you talk such rubbish? Tam and I are jolly good friends. He is a real fine man, as straight as a die and as plucky as he's straight. He has more sense, more judgment—"She was breathless.

"Spare me the catalogue of his virtues," said Elizabeth drily. "I grant he is perfection and therefore unlovable. All that I asked you out of sheer idle curiosity was: How is your friendship to be rounded off?"

Vera was silent. "I shall see him to-night, of course," she said with a fine air of unconcern, "and I hope we shall part the best of friends; but as to his being in love with me, that is nonsense!"

"Of course it is," said Elizabeth soothingly.

"What makes you think he is in love with me?" Vera asked suddenly.

"Symptoms."

"But what symptoms?"

"Well, you are always together. He drops bunches of flowers for you on your birthday."

"Pshaw!" said Vera scornfully. "I thought you had more knowledge of men and women. That is friendship."

"Ha, ha!" laughed Elizabeth politely.

"But honestly," asked Vera, "what makes you think so?"

"I won't tell you any more," said the girl, turning around and tying her hair, "but I will put a straight question to you, my dear; do you love Tam?"

"Of course not," Vera was red; "you are making me very uncomfortable. I tell you he is a good friend of mine and I respect him enormously."

"And you don't love him?"

"Of course I don't love him. What a stupid thing to imagine!"

"Such things have happened," said the girl.

"I have never thought of such a thing," said Vera; "but suppose I did, of course it's an absurd idea, but suppose I did?"

"If I were you and I did," said the girl, "I should tell him so."

"Elizabeth!"

"It sounds bold, doesn't it? But I will tell you why I make that suggestion, because if you don't tell him he won't tell you. You see, my dear, you are a very rich young woman, a very well-educated young woman, you have a social position and a large number of friends. Tam is a self-educated man, with no money and very few prospects and no social position, and, as you say, he is straight and honest—"

"He is the straightest and most honest man in the world," said Vera warmly.

"Well, in those circumstances can't you see, he would no more think of asking for you than he would of calling at Buckingham Palace and demanding the Kohinoor!"

"In America," said Vera, "we haven't those absurd ideas."

"Oh, shucks!" said Elizabeth contemptuously. "You seem to forget I was born in Pennsylvania."

And there the conversation ended, and for the rest of the day Vera was silent and thoughtful, excusing her taciturnity by the fact that she had a lot of packing to do and needed to concentrate her mind upon its performance.

The mortal foe to instinct is reason. They are the negative and positive of mental volition. The man who retains the animal gift of unreasoning divination, preserving that clear power against the handicaps which mind training and education impose, is necessarily psychic, or, as they say in certain Celtic countries, "fey."

Tam went up on patrol flying a new "pup"—a tiny machine powerfully engined, which climbed at an angle of fifty degrees and at a surprising speed. He pushed up through a fog bank at three thousand feet and reached blue skies. His engine was running sweetly, there was just the "give" in his little chaser, the indefinable resilience which a good machine should possess, his guns were in excellent order, his controls worked smoothly, but—

Tam was at a loss how to proceed from that "but."

He turned the nose of the "pup" to earth and planed down to the aerodrome.

Blackie left the machine he was about to take and walked across to Tam.

"Anything wrong?" he asked.

"Weel," replied Tam cautiously, "I'd no' go so far as to say that there's verra much wrong wi' the young fellow."

Blackie looked at him keenly.

"Engines—?"

Tam shook his head.

"No, they were wairking bonnily—there's nothing to complain aboot only I just felt that 'pup' an' Tam was no thinkin' the same way."

"Oh!" said Blackie.

He examined the machine, a new one, with the greatest care, tested the controls, examined and sounded stays and struts and shook his head.

"Take up Bartholomew's machine—he went sick this morning," he said.

Tam superintended the preparation of Lieutenant Bartholomew's "pup" and climbing in gave the signal.

"What's the matter with Tam?"

Thornycroft, a flight commander of 89 A, had strolled across and stood with Blackie watching Tam's tiny machine humming cloudward.

"Tam has what is called on the other side a 'hunch,'" said Blackie; "come and look at this machine and see if you can find anything wrong with it. She's new from the maker," he went on, "in fact, the young gentleman who represents the firm is at this moment in the mess laying down the law on aviation, its past, present and illimitable future—there he is!"

Thornycroft paused in his inspection to watch the newcomer. He was a young man of singular confidence, who talked so very loudly to the officer who accompanied him that the two men by the machine felt themselves included in the conversation long before they could make themselves audible in reply.

"Hello—hello," said Mr. Theodore Mann, "what's wrong— eh?"

"One of my best pilots took her up and didn't like her," said Blackie.

"Didn't like her? What's wrong with her—cold feet, eh? Bless you, they all get it sooner or later—'the pitcher goes often to the well,' et cetera. That's a proverb that every flying man should unlearn, eh?"

He leapt lightly into the machine and jiggled the joy-stick.

"I'll take her up if you don't mind—hi, you!" he called a mechanic, "start her up—ready—contact! Z-r-r-r—!"

The little bird skimmed the smooth floor of the aerodrome and dived upward in a wide circle.

"She's all right," said Thornycroft, shading his eyes; "what's wrong with Tam, I wonder?"

"Tam doesn't funk a thing," protested Blackie, "I've never known him —my God!"

Apparently nothing happened—only the machine without warning buckled up and broke two thousand feet in the air, a wing dropped off and a crumpled thing, which bore no resemblance to an airplane, dropped straight as a plummet to earth.

It fell less than a hundred yards from the aerodrome and Mr. Theodore Mann was dead when they pulled him from the wreckage.

Blackie directed the salvage work and returned a very thoughtful man. When Tam returned from his tour he sent for him.

"You have heard the news, I suppose?"

Tam nodded gravely.

"Now, tell me, Tam," said Blackie, "did you feel anything wrong with the machine—why did you bring her down?"

"Sir-r," said Tam, "I'll no' romance an' A'm tellin' ye Flyin'-Coor truth. I saw nothin' an' felt nothin'—the engines were guid an' sweet an' she swung like a leddy, but—"

"But?"

"Weel, what would ye say if ye were zoomin' up an' of a sudden, for no reason, yeer hair stood up an' yeer flesh went creepy an' yeer mouth grew as dry as Sunday morning? An' there was a cauld, cauld sensation under yeer belt an' the skin aboot yeer eyes was all strained and ye smelt things an' tasted things sharper, as if all yeer senses was racin' like the propeller of a boat when her bow goes under water?"

Blackie shivered. "That's how you felt, eh?" he asked. "Well, you needn't explain further, Tam."

"'Tis the airman's sixty-sixth sense," said Tam. "If he's worried or sad that sixty-sixth sense gets thrown up and becomes more veevid, if ye'll understand me."

"Worried? Sad?" said Blackie quickly. "What's worrying you, Tam? Haven't you had your pay this month?"

Tam smiled slowly. "What that young fellow, Cox, is doing wi' ma fortune doesna keep me awake at nights," he said; "the MacTavishes are feckless, extravagant bodies and it no' concairns me whether ma balance is one poond or two."

"What is worrying you?" asked Blackie.

"Weel," said Tam slowly, "A'm just a wee bit grieved. A frien' o' mine is leaving France."

"Friend of yours?" said Blackie. "Who is your friend?"

"He is a braw big fellow about six foot high wi' muscular arms and curly hair," said Tam. "His name's Jamie Macfarlane, and his mither's a leddy in her own right."

Thus embarked upon his career of mendacity the artist in Tam compelled him to complete the picture.

"We were at school together, Angus and A'."

"You said Jamie just now, Tam," reproved Blackie.

"Angus is his second name," said the glib Tam; "we were brought up in the same village, the village of Glascae, and tramped off to the same college at six every morning when the bummer went. There'd we sit, me and Alec."

"Angus," suggested Blackie.

"Me and Alec Angus Jamie Macfarlane," said the undisturbed Tam, "listenin' wi' eager ears to the discoorses of Professor Ferguson who took the Chair in Rivets at the Govan Iron Works Seminary, drinkin' out of the same mug —"

"Tam, you're lying," said Blackie; "what is really worrying you and who's your friend?"

Tam heaved a sigh. "Ah, weel," he said, "A' shall be wanting to go into Amiens, to-night, Captain Blackie, sir-r, and A've a graund poem at the back of me heid that A'd like to be writing. You'll no' be wanting me?"

"Not till four," said Captain Blackie; "I want you to stand by then in case Fritz tries something funny. The circus paid a visit to 89 yesterday evening and it may be our turn to-night."

Tam closed and locked the door of his room, produced a large pad of writing-paper, an ink-well, and fitted his pen with a new nib before he began his valedictory poem.

Never had a poem been more difficult to write to this ready versifier. He crossed out and rewrote, he destroyed sheet after sheet before the rough work of his hands was ready for polishing.

"How may a puir wee airman fly
When ye have carried off his sky?"

the verse began, and perhaps those were the two most extravagant lines in the farewell verse.

He wrote a fair copy, folded it carefully, inserted it into an envelope and slipped it into his breast pocket. He was to see Vera that night and had no other feeling but one of blank helplessness, for he had neither the right nor the desire to reveal by one word his closely guarded secret, a secret which he fondly believed was shared by none.

His plan was to give her the envelope on the promise that it should not be opened and read until she had reached America. He had invented and carefully rehearsed certain cautious words of farewell, so designed that she might accept them on the spot as conventional expressions of his regret at her leaving, but pondering them afterward, could discover in these simple phrases a hint of his true sentiment.

Such was the difficulty of composition that he was late for parade. All the squadron which was not actually engaged in routine duty was present. Ordinarily they would have been dismissed after the briefest wait, but to- day Blackie kept gunners, observers and pilots standing by their machines.

At half-past four Blackie hurried across from his office. "There's a general alarm," he said. "Everybody is to go up. Tam, take number six and patrol the area."

As the machines rose a big motor-car came flying on to the ground and two staff officers alighted.

Blackie turned and saluted his brigadier. "We only just got the message through, sir," he said.

The general nodded. "It was signalled to me on the road," he said; "I expected it. Who is in charge of that flight?"

"Mr. MacTavish, sir."

"Tam, eh?" The general nodded his approval. "The circus is getting big and bold," he said; "Fritz has a new machine and he is making the most of it. There they come, the beauties!"

He slipped his field-glasses from the case at his belt and focused them upon the sky. The enemy came, a graceful V-shaped flight of monstrous geese, throbbing and humming, and the wandering patrols above changed direction and flew to meet them.

As at a signal the V parted at the fork, each angle divided and subdivided into two, so that where one broad arrow-head had been, were four diamonds. The anti-aircraft guns were staining the evening skies brown and white till the attacking squadrons came gliding like tiny flies into the disturbed area, when the gun-fire ceased.

And now friend and enemy were so mixed that it needed an expert eye to distinguish them. They circled, climbed, dived, looped over and about one another, and it seemed as if the tendency of the oncoming wave was to retire.

"They're going. They've had enough," said the general.

Two machines were wobbling to earth, one in a blaze, whilst a third planed down toward the enemy's lines. The fighters were going farther and farther away, all except three machines that seemed engaged in weaving an invisible thread one about the other.

Under and over, round, up, down, and all the time the ceaseless chatter of machine-guns.

Then one side-slipped, recovered and dropped on his tail to earth. The fight was now between two machines, the maneuvers were repeated, the same knitting of some queer design until—

"Got him!" yelled the general.

The German plane fell in that slow spiral which told its own tale to the expert watchers. Then suddenly his nose went down and he crashed.

"Who's the man? Tam, for a ducat!"

Blackie nodded.

Tam's machine was planing down to earth.

"He'll miss the aerodrome," said the general.

"That's not Tam's way of returning at all," said Blackie with knitted brows.

The machine dropped in the very field where the "Sausage-Killer" had been brought down a week before. It did not skim down but landed awkwardly, swaying from side to side until it came to a stand-still.

Blackie was racing across the field. He reached the machine and took one glance at the pilot. Then he turned to the mechanic who followed at his heels.

"'Phone an ambulance," he said; "they've got Tam at last."

For Tam sat limply in his seat, his chin on his breast, his hand still clasped about the bloody grip of his machine-gun.

The matron beckoned Vera.

"Here's your last job, Vera," she said with a smile. "Take your car to the aerodrome. One of the pilots has been killed."

Vera stared. "At the aerodrome?"

Control it as she might, her voice shook.

"Yes—didn't you see the fight in the air?"

"I came out as it was finishing—oh, may I take the ambulance?"

The matron looked at her in wonder. "Yes, child, take the Stafford car," she nodded to an ambulance which waited on the broad drive.

Without another word Vera ran to the car and cranked it up. As she climbed into the driver's seat she felt her knees trembling.

"Please God, it isn't Tam!" she prayed as she drove the little car along the aerodrome road; "not Tam, dear Lord—not Tam!"

And yet, by the very panic within her she knew it was Tam and none other.

"To the left, I think."

She looked round in affright.

She had been oblivious to the fact that a doctor had taken his seat by her side—it was as though he had emerged from nothingness and had assumed shape and substance as he spoke.

She turned her wheel mechanically, bumped across a little ditch and passed through a broken fence to where a knot of men were regarding something on the ground.

She hardly stopped the ambulance before she leapt out and pushed her way through the group.

"Tam!" she whispered and at that moment Tam opened his eyes. He looked in wonder from face to face, then his eyes rested on the girl.

She was down on her knees by his side in a second and her hand was under his head.

"Tam!" she whispered and thrilled at the look which came into his blue eyes.

Then before them all she bent her head and kissed him.

"From which moment," said Blackie afterward, "Tam began one of the most remarkable recoveries medical science has ever recorded. He had three bullets through his chest, one through his shoulder-blade, and two of his ribs were broken."

Tam closed his eyes. "Vera," he murmured.

She looked up, self-possessed, and eyed Blackie steadily as the doctor stooped over the stricken man on the other side and gingerly felt for the wounds.

"Tam is going to live, Captain Blackie," she said, "because he knows I want him to—don't you, dear?"

"Aye—lassie," said Tam faintly.

"Because—because," she said, "we are going to be married, aren't we, Tam?"

He nodded and she stooped to listen. "Say it—in— Scotch."

She said it—in his ear, her eyes bright and shining, her face as pink as the sunset flooding the scene and then she got up to her feet and they lifted the stretcher and slid it gently into the grooved guides on the floor of the ambulance.

"Now—driver," said the doctor with a little smile.

She went to her place and mounted to the seat. The hands that touched the polished wheel trembled and she slipped back to the ground again, her face white.

"I can't—I can't drive him," she said and burst into tears upon Blackie's shoulder.

So Blackie drove the car himself and left his general to wipe Vera's eyes.

A month later Captain Blackie went to Havre to see Tam en route for home.

"You're a wonderful fellow, Tam—you ought to be dead really instead of being bound for England."

"Scotland," corrected Tam.

"But don't you think you're lucky?"

"Weel," said Tam, "I did until the morn, then I struck a verra bad patch."

"Bad luck," said the innocent and surprised Blackie, "I am sorry to hear that. What happened?"

"The big feller, the principal doctor," said Tam, "said I might smoke a wee seegair, and, believe me, Captain Blackie, sir-r, when I looked in ma pooch there wasna a single—"

Blackie took his cigar-case from his pocket, opened and extended it.

"Tam," he said, "you're nearly well."

Edgar Wallace – A Short Biography

Richard Horatio Edgar Wallace was born on the 1st April 1875 at 7 Ashburnham Grove, Greenwich. His mother, Mary Jane "Polly" Richards was born into an Irish Catholic family in Liverpool in 1843 and had worked in theatres, both as an actress in bit-parts and as a stagehand and usherette, until she married a Merchant Navy Captain, Joseph Richards, in 1867. He too had been born into an Irish Catholic family in Liverpool. His father had also been a Captain in the Merchant Navy, and his mother's family had a marine background. Mary was eight months pregnant with Joseph's child when he died at sea, and it was once the child had been born that she first turned to the stage, taking the stage name Polly Richards.

She joined the Marriott family theatre troupe in 1872. It was managed by Mrs. Alice Edgar, Richard Edgar, Grace Edgar, Adeline Edgar and Richard Horatio Edgar, Wallace's father. In late 1874 Mary and Richard Horatio Edgar had a brief sexual encounter at the party following a successful show, and she fell pregnant. Worried about the scandal which would ensue and fearing that she might forever lose her job at the troupe, she fabricated an obligation in Greenwich would detain her there for at least six months. She lived in a room in the boarding house on Ashburnham Grove until her son, Edgar, was born. She had already made preparations through her midwife for a couple to foster the child, and when Edgar was born the midwife presented her with Mrs Freeman. Her husband was a fishmonger at Billingsgate market and she already had ten children. She was happy to foster the child and for Polly to make frequent visits to see him in exchange for a small sum of money which Polly made from her work in the theatre troupe.

Wallace was now known as Richard Horatio Edgar Freeman, taking his father's forenames and his foster family's surname. Broadly speaking his childhood was a happy one. The Freemans looked after him lovingly and he had good friendships with his foster siblings, particularly Clara Freeman, twenty years his senior, who often looked after him as a child. After a few years Polly's finances tightened and she was no longer in a position to afford the fee she had been paying the Freemans. However, they had grown to love the young Wallace and opted to adopt him in order to keep him out of the workhouse. Polly could no longer visit him. George Freeman was keen to ensure that he had equal opportunities and did all he could to secure him an education at St. Alfege with St. Peter's, a Peckham boarding school. Despite his adoptive father's efforts, though, Wallace left the school aged twelve for truancy.

Instead he went to work and by the time he was fourteen or fifteen he had experience selling newspapers at Ludgate Circus, near Fleet Street, as a worker in a rubber factory, as a shoe shop assistant, as a milk delivery boy and as a ship's cook. He stole from the milk company which resulted in his dismissal, and in 1894 was engaged to a local girl from Deptford named Edith Anstree, though he broke this off and instead joined the Infantry. He adopted the name Edgar Wallace which he took from Lew Wallace, the author of *Ben-Hur*, and his medical record records a diminutive 33" chest and a stunted growth. his first posting was with the West Kent Regiment in South Africa in 1896, though he did not enjoy military life, arranging to be transferred to the Royal Army Medical Corps. Though this was a less strenuous job, it was also significantly less pleasant and so he again transferred to the Press Corps, which he found suited him far better.

He was in Cape Town in 1898 where he met Rudyard Kipling and was inspired to begin writing and publishing poetry and songs. His first collection of ballads, *The Mission that Failed!* and was enough of a success that in 1899 he paid his way out of the armed forces in order to turn to writing full time. His first work was as a war correspondent for Reuters who kept him in Africa to cover the Boer War, and then for the Daily Mail in 1900 and various other periodicals after that. It was while he was in South Africa that he met and married Ivy Maude Caldecott, who was 21 when they married in 1901, despite her Wesleyan missionary father's strong opposition to the union, for several reasons, one of which was that Wallace's writing was not turning quite the profit he had expected it would. *War and Other Poems* and *Writ in Barracks*, both published in 1900, had not proved as popular as his first collection. Eleanor Clare Hellier Wallace, their first child, died of meningitis in 1903 and, in rather deep debt, they returned to London. Wallace used his contacts with the Daily Mail to get work with them in London, electing to write detective novels as a means of making quick money.

Wallace met Polly, his birth mother, in 1903. He didn't remember her from his childhood as he had been too young when she became unable to visit, so it was as though they were meeting for the first time. She was sixty years old and terminally ill, living in abject poverty. She had come to Wallace seeking financial support, but he turned her away. She died in the Bradford Infirmary later that year. In 1904 he and Ivy had a son, Bryan. He was still writing and had completed his first thriller, *The Four Just Men*. Since nobody would publish it he resorted to setting up his own publishing company which he called

Tallis Press and he published a serialised version of *The Four Just Men* in 1905. He received promotional assistance from the Daily Mail in which he ran a competition for entrants to guess the method of murder in the final chapter, with a prize of £1,000 for a correct guess. Although the paper's proprietor, Lord Alfred Harmsworth, refused Wallace the £1,000 prize money, Wallace persisted and went ahead with the competition, recklessly advertising on billboards and buses all over the country, hoping to expand his advertisements across the Empire. His worried colleagues at the Daily Mail managed to convince him to lower the prize money to £500, split into a first prize of £250, a second prize of £200 and a third of £50, but with the total cost of his advertisements nearing £2,000 he would need to sell £2,500 worth of copies before he could see any profit. He was confident that this could be achieved in just three months.

Though he had remarkable enthusiasm, it became clear that his managerial skills left a lot to be desired. It soon emerged that nowhere in the competition terms and conditions had he included a clause limiting the competition to one single winner; instead, any entrant with a winning answer was entitled to their corresponding prize money. Thus, if ten entrants guessed the first prize answer, the competition was obliged to pay each entrant £250. This error was only noticed after the competition had been closed and the solution had been printed in the final installment of the novel, meaning that not only was there no opportunity to write his way out of enormous financial obligation, but the entrants who had guessed correctly would by now have read the final chapter and know they had done so. £250 was an enormous amount of money to the average Edwardian family and those entitled to it were likely to make a lot of noise if they didn't receive their money. Despite this, Wallace's fist instinct was to attempt to ignore the issue entirely, even as he discovered that he initial calculations had been dramatically over-enthusiastic and it would take nearer to two years of continuous sales to break even at the initial cost of £2,500, let alone the new figure which included every correct guesser. Compounding the problem even further was the awful realisation that as sales continued throughout the initial three month period and Wallace approached the £2,500 break-even figure, new readers were still eligible to enter and guess correctly. Though it is unknown how much he eventually owed his readers, Lord Harmsworth found himself having to loan over £5,000 in order to protect the reputation of the newspaper, since 1906 had come around and there still hadn't been a list printed of all prize-winners. It was less a charitable act than one of a man anxious that the failure would reflect ill on his own paper. Wallace filed for bankruptcy shortly thereafter and as a token gesture to his creditors sold the rights to the novel to Sir George Newnes, a publisher and editor, for £75. In the midst of this chaos though, Wallace managed to write and published *Smithy*, which would become the first of a series of *Smithy* novels.

Following this fiascos Wallace was dismissed from the Daily Mail in 1907 when inaccuracies which were found in his reporting, resulting in libel cases being brought against the paper. That year he became the first reporter to be fired from the Daily Mail and was his awful reputation prevented him from finding work at any other papers. Despite all this, though, he travelled to the Congo Free State later that year and reported on the criminal treatment of the Congolese people by King Leopold II of Belgium and the Belgian rubber companies. Up to fifteen million Congolese were killed in various atrocities, and Wallace was asked to serialise stories based on his experiences for her penny magazine *Weekly Tale-Teller*. He and Ivy had another daughter, named Patricia, in 1908. Though his new work for *Weekly Tale-Teller* was bringing in some money, their financial situation was still dire and Ivy was occasionally forced to sell off her jewellery and possessions in order to pay for food. In 1911 his Congolese stories were published in a collection called *Sanders of the River*, which quickly became a bestseller. He would publish eleven more such collections featuring a total of 102 stories of adventure and tribal life set on the river Congo.

From 1908 he started to enjoy a revival of both his success and his reputation. The majority of his initial writing he sold outright in order to make money as quickly as possible and placate his creditors in the

United Kingdom and South Africa, but as his success saw the reestablishment of his reputation he began to find work once again as a journalist, beginning in horse racing for the *Week-End*, the *Evening News* and then as an editor for the *Week-End Racing Supplement*. Following this success he started his own racing papers, *Bibury's* and *R. E. Walton's Weekly*, eventually buying his own racehorses and losing thousands gambling. His success was insufficient to support his newly extravagant lifestyle and his marriage began to fail in the light of his financial irresponsibility. He and Ivy had their last child together, Michael Blair Wallace, in 1916, and she filed for divorce in 1918 moving to Tunbridge Wells with her children.

Wallace began to fall for his secretary Ethel Violet King and they married in 1921, having a child, Penelope Wallace, in 1923, who would herself go on to become a successful crime writer. Wallace now began to take his career as a fiction writer more seriously, signing with Hodder and Stoughton in 1921. He now began to organize his contracts more carefully, arranging for royalties and properly organized promotions, run by people more business-minded than himself. He was marketed as the 'King of Thrillers' and they gave him the trademark image of a trilby, a cigarette holder and a yellow Rolls Royce. He was truly prolific, capable not only of producing a 70,000 word novel in three days but of doing three novels in a row in such a manner. His publishers signed off on almost everything he wrote as soon as he turned it in, estimating that by 1928 one in four books being read at any time was written by Wallace, for alongside his famous thrillers he wrote variously in other genres, including but not limited to science fiction, non-fiction accounts of WWI which amounted to ten volumes and screen plays. Eventually he would reach the remarkable total of 170 novels, 18 stage plays and 957 short stories.

Wallace became chairman of the Press Club which to this day holds an annual Edgar Wallace Award, rewarding 'excellence in writing'. In 1923 he broadcasted a report on the Epsom Derby horse race for the British Broadcasting Company, making him the first ever radio sports correspondent. His ex-wife Ivy had suffered from breast cancer between 1923-1924, and it eventually killed her in 1926 despite a successful operation to remove a tumour the year before. He wrote the essay "The Canker in our Midst" in 1926 which dealt, aggressively and controversially, with the problem of paedophilia in show business, describing how children were unwittingly left open to sexual abuse, and linking paedophilia with homosexuality. Its tone has been described as "intolerant, blustering, kick-the-blighters-down-the-stairs". He was appointed chairman of the British Lion Film Corporation on the back of the success of *The Ringer* and on the agreement that he give British Lion first choice on all his future work. This contract gave him an annual salary and a large amount of stock with the company, along with a stipend on all British Lion production of his work and 10% of their annual profits. This extraordinary contract gave him annual earnings by 1929 of almost £50,000, or almost £2 million in 2014.

He now became an active figure in politics, entering the 1931 general election as a Liberal contestant in Blackpool, rejecting the current government in favour of free trade. He lost the election by over 33,000 votes and went to America in late 1931, once again deeply in debt after buying the *Sunday News* which closed six months later. In America he quickly found work as a script doctor for RKO Pictures, enjoying early success with the 1932 adaptation of *The Hound of the Baskervilles*. This success, along with that of the play *The Green Pack*, established his reputation in America and he was able to see his own work adapted for film, beginning with *The Four Just Men*. His most successful theatrical work, *On The Spot*, which explores the life of Al Capone, has been described as "arguably, in construction, dialogue, action, plot and resolution, still one of the finest and purest of 20th-century melodramas". These successes led to his assignation on RKO's "gorilla picture" which would become famous as King Kong in 1933.

He worked on the first draft though he was beginning to experience severe headaches which brought about a diagnosis of diabetes. Despite taking medication to address his condition, it deteriorated in a matter of days. His wife booked him passage home but soon heard that he had entered a coma and died of his condition and double pneumonia on the 7th of February 1932 in North Maple Drive, Beverly Hills. In his honour the bell at St. Bride's church on Fleet Street tolled for the duration of the morning while the flags flew at half-mast. He was buried near his home in England at Chalklands, Bourne End, in Buckinghamshire. Once again, at the time of his death he was in severe debt, mostly to racing bookkeepers, though these debts were settled within two years thanks to the enormous royalties his estate continued to receive from his contracts. His writing has been translated into 29 languages, and is considered one of the most important bodies of Colonial writing.

Edgar Wallace – A Concise Bibliography

African Novels
Sanders of the River (1911)
The People of the River (1911)
The River of Stars (1913)
Bosambo of the River (1914)
Bones (1915)
The Keepers of the King's Peace (1917)
Lieutenant Bones (1918)
Bones in London (1921)
Sandi the Kingmaker (1922)
Bones of the River (1923)
Sanders (1926)
Again Sanders (1928)

Four Just Men (Series)
The Four Just Men (1905)
The Council of Justice (1908)
The Just Men of Cordova (1917)
The Law of the Four Just Men (US title: Again the Three Just Men) (1921)
The Three Just Men (1926)
Again the Three Just Men (US title: The Law of the Three Just Men) (1929) a.k.a. Again the Three

Mr. J. G. Reeder (Series)
Room 13 (1924)
The Mind of Mr. J. G. Reeder (US title: The Murder Book of Mr. J. G. Reeder) (1925)
Terror Keep (1927)
Red Aces (1929)[27]
The Guv'nor and Other Short Stories (US title: Mr. Reeder Returns) (1932)

Detective Sgt. (Inspector) Elk series
The Nine Bears or The Other Man or The Cheaters (1910)
revised as Silinski - Master Criminal (1930)
The Fellowship of the Frog (1925)
The Joker or The Colossus (1926)

The Twister (1928)
The India-Rubber Men (1929)
White Face (1930)

Educated Evans (Series)
Educated Evans (1924)
More Educated Evans (1926)
Good Evans (1927)

Smithy (Series)
Smithy (1905)
Smithy Abroad (1909)
Smithy and The Hun (1915)
Nobby or Smithy's Friend Nobby (1916)

Crime Novels
Angel Esquire (1908)
The Fourth Plague or Red Hand (1913)
Grey Timothy or Pallard the Punter (1913)
The Man Who Bought London (1915)
The Melody of Death (1915)
A Debt Discharged (1916)
The Tomb of T'Sin (1916)
The Secret House (1917)
The Clue of the Twisted Candle (1918)
Down under Donovan (1918)
The Man Who Knew (1918)
The Strange Lapses of Larry Loman (1918)
The Green Rust (1919)
Kate Plus Ten (1919)
The Daffodil Mystery or The Daffodil Murder (1920)
Jack O'Judgment (1920)
The Angel of Terror or The Destroying Angel (1922)
The Crimson Circle (1922)
Mr. Justice Maxwell or Take-A-Chance Anderson(1922)
The Valley of Ghosts (1922)
Captains of Souls (1923)
The Clue of the New Pin (1923)
The Green Archer (1923)
The Missing Million (1923)
The Dark Eyes of London or The Croakers (1924)
Double Dan or Diana of Kara-Kara (US Title) (1924)
The Face in the Night or The Diamond Men or The Ragged Princess (1924)
The Sinister Man (1924)
The Three Oak Mystery (1924)
The Blue Hand or Beyond Recall (1925)
The Daughters of the Night (1925)
The Gaunt Stranger or Police Work (1925) revised as The Ringer (1926)

A King by Night (1925)
The Strange Countess (1925)
The Avenger or The Hairy Arm (1926)
'The Black Abbot (1926)
The Day of Uniting (1926)
The Door with Seven Locks (1926)
The Man from Morocco or Souls In Shadows or The Black (US Title) (1926)
The Million Dollar Story (1926)
The Northing Tramp or The Tramp (1926)
Penelope of the Polyantha (1926)
The Square Emerald or The Woman (1926)
The Terrible People or The Gallows' Hand (1926)
We Shall See! or The Gaol-Breakers (US Title) (1926)
The Yellow Snake or The Black Tenth (1926)
Big Foot (1927)
The Feathered Serpent or Inspector Wade or Inspector Wade and the Feathered Serpent (1927)
Flat 2 (1927)
The Forger or The Counterfeiter (1927)
Terror Keep (1927)
The Hand of Power or The Proud Sons of Ragusa (1927)
The Man Who Was Nobody (1927)
Number Six (1927)
The Squeaker or The Sign of the Leopard or The Squealer (US Title) (1927)
The Traitor's Gate (1927)
The Double (1928)
The Flying Squad (1928)
The Gunner or Gunman's Bluff (US Title) (1928)
Four Square Jane or The Fourth Square (1929)
The Golden Hades or Stamped In Gold or The Sinister Yellow Sign (1929)
The Green Ribbon (1929)
The Calendar (1930)
The Clue of the Silver Key or The Silver Key (1930)
The Lady of Ascot (1930)
The Devil Man or Sinister Street or Silver Steel
or The Life and Death of Charles Peace (1931)
The Man at the Carlton or The Mystery of Mary Grier (1931)
The Coat of Arms or The Arranways Mystery (1931)
On the Spot: Violence and Murder in Chicago (1931)
When the Gangs Came to London or Scotland Yard's Yankee Dick
or The Gangsters Come To London (1932)
The Frightened Lady or The Case of the Frightened Lady or Criminal At Large (1933)
The Green Pack (1933)
The Man Who Changed His Name (1935)
The Mouthpiece (1935)
Smoky Cell (1935)
The Table (1936)
Sanctuary Island (1936)

Other Novels
Captain Tatham of Tatham Island or Eve's Island or The Island of Galloping Gold (1909)
The Duke in the Suburbs (1909)
Private Selby (1912)
"1925" - The Story of a Fatal Peace (1915)
Those Folk of Bulboro (1918)
The Book of all Power (1921)
Flying Fifty-five (1922)
The Books of Bart (1923)
Barbara on Her Own (1926)

Poetry Collections
The Mission That Failed (1898)
War and Other Poems (1900)
Writ In Barracks (1900)

Non-Fiction
Unofficial Despatches of the Anglo-Boer War (1901)
Famous Scottish Regiments (1914)
Field Marshal Sir John French (1914)
Heroes All: Gallant Deeds of the War (1914)
The Standard History of the War – Volumes 1 – 4 (1914)
Kitchener's Army and the Territorial Forces:
The Full Story of a Great Achievement (1915)
Vol. 2-4. War of the Nations (1915)
Vol. 5-7. War of the Nations (1916)
Vol. 8-9. War of the Nations (1917)
Famous Men and Battles of the British Empire (1917)
Tam of the Scouts (1918)
The Real Shell-Man: The Story of Chetwynd of Chilwell (1919)
People or Edgar Wallace by Himself(1926)
The Trial of Patrick Herbert Mahon (1928)
My Hollywood Diary (1932)

Screenplays
King Kong (1932, first draft of original screenplay, 110 pages) While the script was not used in its entirety, much of it was retained for the final screenplay.
The Hound of the Baskervilles (1932, British film)
The Squeaker (1930, British film)
Prince Gabby (1929, British film)
Mark of the Frog (1928, American film)
The Valley of Ghosts (192

Short Story Collections
The Admirable Carfew (1914)
The Adventure of Heine (1917)
Tam O' the Scouts (1918)
The Fighting Scouts (1919)

Chick (1923)
The Black Avons (1925)
The Brigand (1927)
The Mixer (1927)
This England (1927)
The Orator (1928)
The Thief in the Night (1928)
Elegant Edward (1928)
The Lone House Mystery and Other Stories (1929)
The Governor of Chi-Foo (1929)
Again the Ringer The Ringer Returns (US Title) (1929)
The Big Four or Crooks of Society (1929)
The Black or Blackmailers I Have Foiled (1929)
The Cat-Burglar (1929)
Circumstantial Evidence (1929)
Fighting Snub Reilly (1929)
For Information Received (1929)
Forty-Eight Short Stories (1929)
Planetoid 127 and The Sweizer Pump (1929)
The Ghost of Down Hill & The Queen of Sheba's Belt (1929)
The Iron Grip (1929)
The Lady of Little Hell (1929)
The Little Green Man (1929)
The Prison-Breakers (1929)
The Reporter (1929)
Killer Kay (1930)
Mrs William Jones and Bill (1930)
Forty Eight Short-Stories (1930)
The Stretelli Case and Other Mystery Stories (1930)
The Terror (1930)
The Lady Called Nita (1930)
Sergeant Sir Peter or Sergeant Dunn, C.I.D. (1932)
The Scotland Yard Book of Edgar Wallace (1932)
The Steward (1932)
Nig-Nog and other humorous stories (1934)
The Last Adventure (1934)
The Woman From the East (1934) Co-written By Robert George Curtis
The Edgar Wallace Reader of Mystery and Adventure (1943)
The Undisclosed Client (1963)

Other
King Kong, with Draycott M. Dell, (1933), 28 October 1933 Cinema Weekly

Plays
An African Millionaire (1904)
The Forest of Happy Dreams (1910)
Dolly Cutting Herself (1911)
The Manager's Dream (1914)

M'Lady (1921)
Double Dan (1926)
The Mystery of room 45 (1926)
A Perfect Gentleman (1927)
The Terror (1927)
Traitors Gate (1927)
The Lad (1928)
The Man Who Changed His Name (1928)
The Squeaker (1928)
The Calendar (1929)
Persons Unknown (1929)
The Ringer (1929)
The Mouthpiece (1930)
On the Spot (1930)
Smoky Cell (1930)
The Squeaker (1930)
To Oblige A Lady (1930)
The Case of the Frightened Lady (1931)
The Old Man (1931)
The Green Pack (1932)
The Table (1932)

www.ingramcontent.com/pod-product-compliance
Lightning Source LLC
Chambersburg PA
CBHW071414170626
46811CB00003B/1402